Isaac Mast

The Gun, Rod and Saddle; or, Nine Months in California

Isaac Mast

The Gun, Rod and Saddle; or, Nine Months in California

ISBN/EAN: 9783337158439

Printed in Europe, USA, Canada, Australia, Japan

Cover: Foto ©Andreas Hilbeck / pixelio.de

More available books at **www.hansebooks.com**

THE

Gun, Rod and Saddle;

OR,

NINE MONTHS IN CALIFORNIA.

BY

REV. ISAAC MAST, A. M.

PHILADELPHIA:
METHODIST EPISCOPAL BOOK AND PUBLISHING HOUSE,
1018 ARCH STREET.
REV. J. B. McCULLOUGH, AGENT.
1875.

PREFACE.

THE following pages are almost wholly the record of personal experience. Descending to a detail that would be trivial to the majority of adult readers, they are suited mainly to youth. There are no battles fought, no discoveries made, no mines developed. The great busy world has no time for small matters. And yet there are subjects referred to, in which some persons of more advanced years are interested.

Two objects are aimed at, viz: To furnish instructive entertainment for our young people, who are always reading; and to encourage some desponding invalid not to give up the struggle.

3

In the work of a regular itinerant minister, in December, 1871, the author was suddenly stricken down with typhoid pneumonia, and left vocally disabled. Having slowly recovered during the following year, in December, 1872, he sailed for California. There he lived and hunted in the mountains, rode over the plains, and fished in the streams, until the following October, when he came back, resumed partial labor, and in the spring of 1875, took full work.

He believes that many die before their time —that if personal experience were more closely observed, than the restricted advice of unskillful physicians; if patent medicines were severely let alone; if exposure was risked and exertion dared, then would many tombs, many years longer await their occupants.

It is hoped that a review of the writer's experience may prove as healthful to others, as the actual exercise was to himself.

I. M.

Roxborough, Phila., Oct., 1875.

CONTENTS.

CHAPTER I.

ON THE WAY.

Sea Birds—Marvelous Eating—Color of the Sea—Entering the Bay—A Song spoiled—Scene at the Wharf—Aspinwall—Palms—Vultures—Statues—Churches—Jelly-fish—Railroad to Panama—Wood Chopping—Scant Clothing—Panama—Cathedral—A Coffin Making—School—A Broken Sabbath—Amingo Island—Ants—Wise Crabs—The Pacific—Fire in the Sea—Christmas—Volcanoes—The Captain and Sabbath service—Acapulco—Early Attack—The Town—Market—Garden—Diver—Sights in the Sea—Manzanillo—The Disabled Ship—The "Costa Rica" in tow—San Diego—The little "Gipsy"—A Mirage—Seal Rocks—The Golden Gate—On Land.   11

CHAPTER II.

SAN FRANCISCO TO VISALIA.

Summer in Winter—A Solid City—The Chinese Question—Preachers' Meeting—The Bay—Oakland—Night ride to Goshen—Stage to Visalia—The Town—"Betsy" after game—

5

Squirrels—Quail—Rabbits—Jacket and Pantaloons—Hare—
Wild-ducks—Scaly success—The Misletoe—Weather—The
Sierra Nevadas—Sun-rise—Sun-set—Off for the Mountains. 49

CHAPTER III.

AMONG THE SIERRAS—GROUSE VALLEY.

The Outfit—Company—Grand Mountain view—A good
Shot—Sky room—Rain and snow—The Hunter's cabin—Grouse
Valley—Cabin and Furniture—"Bridget" at heavy discount—
Game—Snow—Low Temperature—Visit to Cahoon's—Deer
tracks—A five days' hunt—The three-barrelled rifle—Three deer
killed—"Betsy" luckless—Music of the Kaweah—The old adobe
—Contents of packs—The "Parson" poisoned—How "not to
do it"—Farming—Rumbo and the foxes—A dead shot—A wild-
cat—Hooking Suckers—Change of base.　　　　　　69

CHAPTER IV.

AMONG THE SIERRAS—CAHOON'S.

Cabin and Furniture—A day's fishing—Homer—A Panther—
A bear and not a bear—Compromise—Old hunters luckless—
Wild flowers—Literature—Domestic employments—A Mountain
Sabbath—Milking—Washing dishes—Sand-hill Cranes—Rattle
Snakes.—Tarantulas—Mason spider—Lizards—Lake trout—
Grouse—A receipt—Bear tracks—Logs and boulders—An Expe-
dition alone—A dangerous ford—Nine deer—A night in a "big
tree."—"Betsy's" first deer—Tracks of a Grizzly—The log and
boulder quarry—A wonderful flower—A big camp-fire—Hasty
moving—Safe return—Second expedition—The horse "Gimlet"

—Boring through brush—View from a summit—A lone Mallard—Mosquitoes—One deer—A bear after "Me and Betsy"—Polite conduct—Another bear—A ride proposed—The Bible and Canteen.   93

CHAPTER V.

THE BIG TREES.

Timber in California—The Red-woods—Cutting and sawing them—Miles of logs—Felling a Red-wood—"The Big Trees," proper—Tulare Grove—The "General Grant"—"The Old Maid"—"Adam"—"Napoleon"—"General Lee"—Tall Stories—The Mariposa Grove—The "La Fayette"—"The Fallen Giant"—"The Grizzly Giant"—A night under his arm—The Calaveras Grove—Fresno Grove—Australian "Big Trees." 138

CHAPTER VI.

YOSEMITE.

Trail to Paragoy's—Sentinel Dome—Glacier Point—Yosemite Fall—Half Dome—Cap of Liberty—Nevada Fall—Vernal Fall—View to the West—To the bottom—Mirror Lake—Royal Arches—Toys from "Noah's Ark"—Steep trail—Night—Trout at and after breakfast—Fourth of July—Through the Valley—El Capitan—Anecdote of Niagara—Two modes of measuring El Capitan—Too oppressive—"Confounded liars"—Impressions of Yosemite.   157

CHAPTER VII.

THE GEYSERS.

A Sabbath at Garrote—A drunken priest—Fast driving—

Wreck of a Stage—Miraculous Escape—Pluton Creek—Geyser
Canyon—Sulphur Springs—"The Devil's Pulpit"—"The
Witches' Caldron"—"The Devil's Apothecary Shop"—"The
Devil's Grist Mill"—Prompt Exit—New Stage Road to Clover-
dale.   177

CHAPTER VIII.

MENDOCINO.

Extent and Character of Mendocino county—End of a long
ride—Little Lake Valley—Mountain Trout—Wretched luck—
Among the red-woods—A "two-pounder,"—Shooting Salmon
Trout—Unexpected immersion—A four days' hunt.—"Spanish
George"—Two Deer—Little Fawn—Mr. B. in luck—"Betsy" and
I useless—More fish—Tussle with a big Trout—Crippled deer—
Practice with rifle—Importance of a dog—Carter's "bad luck"
—Another hunt—One Deer—Hard scratching—The Orphan
Fawn—Gray Squirrels—Wild Pigeons—Weather—Schools and
Churches—Estimate of human life—Remarkable traits of Char-
acter—Indians—Condition on the Reservations.   187

CHAPTER IX.

SOUTHERN CALIFORNIA.

By Steamer to San Pedro—The "Saints" in a fog—Sinners
in trouble—Santa Barbara—The old Mission—Beautiful Sea
Weeds—"Sinking Peter"—Wilmington—Compton—Florence
—Los Angeles—A ride through the country—" Paradise Re-

gained "—Not yet—To San Bernardino—San Gabriel—Cuca-
monga—The Vintage—The "Mocker"—Opinions—The
Desert—Mt. San Bernardino—The Valley—The Town—Mor-
mons—Ride through the country—An old Schoolmate—Sabbath
—Back to Los Angeles—A run off—The Frenchman and Whis-
ky—Sketch of a horse by Jehu—San Beneventura—"Bull
fight"—"Bearing the Cross"—Staging by water—Climate of
Los Angeles and Santa Barbara—The Santa Inez Mountain—The
River—Luis Obispo—Salinas River and Plain—Return to San
Francisco.   217

CHAPTER X.

HOMEWARD.

By Central Pacific Railroad—Lathrop—A Grizzly Bear—Sac-
ramento—Rocklin—Colfax—Summit—Cape Horn—Truckee—
Snow sheds—Snow-plows—Wadsworth—Virginia City—White
Plains—Mirage Lake—Humboldt Lake and River—Promontory
Point, where the Central Pacific and the Union Pacific unite—
Great Salt Lake—Ogden – Salt Lake City—The Mormons—
Weber Canyon—Thousand Mile Tree—Echo Canyon—The
runaway cars and the wrecked Dutchmen—The Rocky Moun-
tains—Creston—Lake Como—Short-legged Cat-fish—Artesian
Wells—Antelopes—Sherman—Pike's Peak—Cheyenne—Gree-
ley and Denver City—Grand Duke Alexis—Prairie Dog City—
North Platte—Sabbath—Scene in a Railroad Car—Sidney—
Sharp Practice—Platte River—Omaha and Council Bluffs—St.
Louis—Splendid Bridge—Vastness of the country—Home. 241

CHAPTER XI.

WHAT LUCK.

Catching a cold—Two results—Information, health, climate—Irrigation—Frequent poverty—Advantages of Southern California—Difficulties—Fruitful capital—Large farms—Cattle and sheep—"John" in the mines—The Jeweled sorceress—Wrecks on the coast—The good alone rewarded—Effect of climate upon invalids—Advice from experience—A prescription for vocal difficulty. 272

THE

GUN, ROD AND SADDLE.

CHAPTER I.

ON THE WAY.

"CHARLEY, what kind of a bird is that?"

"That? That is a Say-bird, sir."

It was the 18th of December. We were in the middle of the Caribbean Sea, and had not seen a bird after leaving New York Bay. I was leaning on the rail near my state-room door, looking into the mystery of the waves, had noticed this brown-backed bird sweeping around our ship, and as our table-boy passed, having previously learned from him that he had been often at sea since his voyage from Erin,

11

I made a serious inquiry for information. He answered my question most respectfully. He deserved, and a day later, at Aspinwall, received a silver coin, chiefly for that excellent reply.

Just north of Cuba I had seen birds—birds that looked like silver swallows, rising from the waves, flying swiftly from fifty to one hundred yards, then alighting. A riddle followed. Where were they? The sea was rough, and I thought they must be some kind of petrel, at home on the waves. Presently some started and disappeared near the ship. The riddle was answered. They were flying-fish. They are a curious connecting link between the finny tribes in the deeps below, and the winged families of the deeps above.

But some of the inhabitants of our ship, were to me as much of a mystery as the strangers of the sea.

We had rough weather. Most of us could eat little or nothing for some days, and what little we did get down seemed to multiply indefinitely when it had to come up.

Neptune levied a tribute, and all the pow-
ers above and below conspired to see it
paid. But he appeared to have a few favorites
who were exempted. A man next me at table
was one of them. The first smell of salt-water
whetted his appetite. The gale proved a
grindstone. As we got more sick, he got
more hungry. His ability at the table was
simply marvelous. To illustrate. He had
made a bet with some boon companions and
won it. A treat followed. He came to dinner under the influence of liquor. He apolo-
gized, first to me, then to some ladies opposite,
for being in the condition he was, and then
fell to eating. On my first Circuit I had once
helped a stout boy of fourteen, in the absence
of his father from the supper table. I thought
his eating was serious, when he reached his
plate for the fourth piece of long sausage.
But here was a man of medium size, who far
excelled him. After soup, he paid no attention to courses. Remarking to me that his
appetite had been constantly improving since
he came on board, he began with a plate of

pickles. Having finished them, he attacked a glass of celery, sometimes striking, and as often missing the salt-cellar, by his plate. Then followed a dish of "fritters," five in number. Then an "onion stew." Then "corned beef and cabbage." When he ordered "boiled mutton," I left. Subsequently, I learned that he finished with a plate of pudding, over which his unsteady hands had emptied the entire contents of the sauce-boat. The opinion that "Man wants but little here below" is not sustained by all the facts.

Land hove dimly into sight, early in the afternoon of the eighth day from New York. Heavy swells were running twice as fast as we, from North-east to South-west. The color of the sea had changed. The Atlantic looked inky black. Now the water was dark green, and sometimes light blue. In conversation with an old sea captain, now on his way to the Pacific Coast, I asked what caused the changes in appearance? He replied, positively, that they were "Caused by the change of temperature, resulting from the

Gulf Stream flowing around the west end of Cuba." The landsman asked no more questions.

At six o'clock we swept into the little bay at Aspinwall. A dozen or more vessels of various nationalities were lying at anchor. Officers and men were all on deck, and the flags were gayly flying. The bay was smooth as a mirror, the evening beautiful, and all our passengers, steerage excepted, were on the upper deck. On the starboard quarter, a man was using the lead.

Captain Gray, a quiet, old gentleman, stood on the wheel-house, from time to time calling to the men at the wheel, "Starboard!" "Port!" "Steady!"

The man with the lead had a powerful pair of lungs, and this was a grand opportunity to use them. So in a most incomprehensible, sing-song way, he kept calling out, "B-y the m-a-a-r-k eight h-a-a-l-f!" "B-y the m-a-a-r-k f-i-i-i-i-v-e! etc."

The passengers were amused. All conversation ceased, to hear the wondrous song, which steadily lengthened as the depth decreased. The Captain lost his patience, turned toward the noisy man, and shouted down:

"Quit your bawling, sir, and tell us how much water we have."

"Five fathoms, sir," was the prompt reply.

The music ceased. The information was divested of all operatic gymnastics, and was easily understood. I thought of pulpits and choirs that might learn a lesson from the testy order of our long-suffering Captain. Less noise, more definite information.

Our good ship, the Henry Chauncey, swung up to the wharf, and her huge paddle-wheels ceased to revolve. Night and day we had felt the throb of her fifteen hundred horse-power engine, and I had often watched the curious mechanical contrivance that registered her twelve foot strokes. It now marked one hundred and eighteen thousand, seven hundred and five revolutions. The distance run in eight days and six hours was about nineteen hundred and forty miles.

A lively scene now presented itself. The

gangways were placed, and the discharge of freight commenced fore and aft. Such a mixture of men! Negroes, mulattoes, quadroons, octaroons, Creoles, Chinese, white English, mixed Spanish, officers, porters, foremen, hurrying and shouting, talking in several languages, the lowing of young cattle being transferred to the cars, the rumble of barrows, the creaking of pulleys, and the puffing of a spunky little donkey-engine, made up a sight and a sound never to be forgotten. The lanterns gleamed, and the boxes tumbled in the great freight depot, until I was fast asleep.

In the morning a company of us strolled through the town. The streets are regular, wide, unpaved; the houses are mostly one story, some two and three. The better ones only, are built of brick or stone. Some of the officers and employés of the railroad and steamship companies have handsome residences, and many choice flowers adorn their tastefully arranged door-yards. Most of the buildings in the city are roofed with tile; many of the poorer ones, thatched with palm-leaf. The inhabitants are as various as was the throng at the wharf. They were dressed in light summer garb, though it was the twentieth of December. The Thermometer rose to 85° before noon. None of the small children were encumbered with more than a loose slip, and many of them played around among the chickens and domestic animals entirely naked. A few were badly formed, others were perfect models of symmetry. Being of a chocolate color, some of the little fellows looked as if made of mahogany, turned and polished in a turning-lathe.

The flags of different nations were flying over their respective Consulates. Various wares filled numerous large shops on the main street. Oranges, limes, bananas, and pine-apples, loaded the fruit stands. And gamblers with their little tables, dice, and piles of silver half-dollars, were as numerous as the venders of fruit. All the natives gamble, and the man who does not, is, to them, a curiosity. The most beautiful object, one which I had long wished to see, is the palm. There are

said to be one hundred and sixty-five species
in Columbia alone, though only a few are seen
here. They are all graceful in the extreme.
Some of the cocoa palms lift their plumed
crests above the highest buildings, and green
forever, they stand a perpetual emblem of the
tropics. Alongside one of the streets is a
handsome bronze statue of Columbus, by
Thalberg. It is in an unworthy location,
without enclosure, and without elevation.
There is a fine granite monument to the
Messrs. Chauncey, Stephens, and Aspinwall,
on the triangular die of which appear, in alto
relievo, the respective busts of those gentlemen.

Near the north beach is the Episcopal
Church, erected by the company. It is a neat
gothic structure, built of brown stone, brought
from the North. The once handsome interior
was looking badly, the peculiar climate was
making inroads upon the brown stone without,
and an air of pending desolation reigned about
the place. A rector was no longer employed,

and so far as I could learn, there was no Protestant religious service in the city.

Just to the south-east was a small Roman Catholic Church. On the peak of its red tile roof, quietly sitting side by side, were more than a score of buzzards, or vultures. But that was no disgrace to the church, however suggestive it might be, for these birds are very numerous, have the freedom of the city, mingle with the domestic fowls and children, and are really serviceable as scavengers.

In one of the lagoons formed by the incoming tide, I saw a beautiful jelly-fish, just beneath the surface of the water. He looked like an inverted glass bowl, beautiful in form, and almost transparent. I tried to catch him with my umbrella, but he soon got out of my reach by a motion very similar to the opening and shutting of the machine with which I was trying to catch him.

In the same pool, in striking contrast with the jelly-fish, were some black pigs, with the longest legs and noses I ever saw appended to swine. They were gathering roots and

shell-fish. As the tide rose, they stuck to
their work with genuine pig-headedness. And
if Darwin's development theory is correct, it is
not marvelous how their legs and noses became so long. They were evidently in a fair
way to become either cranes or divers.

At one o'clock we were aboard the cars and
steaming out for Panama: distance, forty-
seven miles. There are some respectable hills,
but no high mountains along the road. The
grade is very easy, the road single track, well
laid, and mostly ballasted with stone. The ties
are made of mahogany, as it is the only wood
that resists the terrible depredations of the
ants. The same enemy destroyed the telegraph poles. To meet and defeat them, at
that point, they moulded poles, or rather pillars of cement. These are about twelve feet
high, one foot in diameter at the bottom and
eight inches at top.

Owing to the sickliness of the climate, this
road cost millions of money, and tens of thousands of human lives. As I stood sometimes
upon the rear platform, and looked at those

miles of dark ties over which we were thundering, each one seemed to turn into a dead laborer.   But the wheels of trade do not stop for life.

The cars are very plain, solid plank seats, and about as uncomfortable as the poorest emigrant cars here north.   Fortunately the passage is short, though the fare seemed quite long enough for those who did not have through tickets.   It was twenty-five dollars, gold.

I had expected to see many beautiful flowers and birds.   There were neither.   Only a few of each, and both very plain.   Upon the reeds in a swamp were some black-birds, like those in our own meadows.

There is some good timber, plenty of wood, and nearly all the way, a dense jungle.   Many of the large trees were covered with moss, immense festoons of which swayed in the air, and often hung nearly to the ground.

The population seemed very sparse, and the slight houses were built of poles, interwoven and thatched with palm leaves or reeds.

We saw some of the natives getting out

wood. Instead of an axe, they used a heavy knife about eighteen inches long. With this they slash a path through the jungle, chop the small trees into pieces about two feet long, and then pack them on their little ponies. For this purpose, they have pads made of reeds coming well down the horse's sides. The wood is laid horizontally against these, under straps or ropes, and piled clear up over his back. The load is then strapped tightly to him, and he is ready to take the trail to market.

We passed a native who seemed to be traveling. He had on a hat, a shirt, and a *cigar.* That was all. Indeed, we saw some smoking cigarettes, who had not even a hat. No wagons or wagon roads were to be seen. There were some fields of bananas. These are planted in rows like Indian corn, but eight or ten feet apart. Those we saw were about eight feet high, and seemed to be in bearing condition.

At five o'clock, we reached Panama, got aboard the little transport, and were taken to the steamer, which lay at anchor two or three miles out in the bay. All freight has to be transferred by lighters.

On Saturday, a company of us returned and visited the city. The dilapidated wall toward the sea, and the tile roofs on the generally low buildings within, give the place anything but an imposing appearance. The streets are narrow, but many of them are well paved with cobblestones, and clean. Situated on a bluff, as the city is, the frequent heavy rains wash it thoroughly.

Panama is the centre of considerable trade. Numerous large stores were filled with vast quantities of fancy and useful articles. There were two Protestant, and numerous Catholic churches. Three of these we visited, including the Cathedral on the plaza. They were all in a very untidy condition. Wax figures and gaudy tinsel supplied the place of anything really valuable. The Cathedral, itself, was verging close upon ruin. In the crumbling tower were several old bells, and in niches in front, some wooden Apostles, painted to look like bronze. Unable to gain admission in front, we went to a side door, and in answer to our knocks and calls, an old Creole projected his gray head from a little window up in the tower, and croaked something in Spanish. After waiting a few minutes, the door grated on its rusty hinges, and we were admitted. Making our way over piles of damp rubbish, by another little door, we were ushered into the main audience room. It is cruciform, and probably seventy by ninety feet. Large portions of the marble floor are taken up with memorial slabs. Numerous tablets are also let into the walls and pillars. Some of them are very fine marble, and really handsome; all the inscriptions are in Spanish. The whole place was sadly neglected, and seemed better fitted for a sepulchre than for a church. Indeed, no service had been held there, we were informed, for more than two years. There were large holes in the lofty roof, through which torrents of rain had poured. In the east transept, the cray-fish had worked up bushels of earth between the poorly fitting flag-stones and memorial slabs. It looked as though the dead beneath might be getting impatient for a resurrection. The sexton had left us to roam at will; and he safely might, for had we been thieves, there was nothing worth stealing. He reappeared, however, with a metal plate containing some silver coins, which were disposed upon it like a few hot cakes, when necessity for show, at a hotel, exceeds the supply. We added a few to his store—enough to pay for washing his poor garments, and repairing the wretched slippers which he shoved over the floor with his naked feet.

On a little recess stood an empty wine bottle, and in some remote corner, up near the roof, we heard the sound of a carpenter's saw.

With the dead beneath, the wine of life all gone, that ghost of a sexton and gloom around, it seemed as though the carpenter were making a coffin to bury the whole institution. Surely anything so far decomposed were better in the grave than out of it.

We visited a school, also. A pleasant little man had charge of about thirty children. We

were courteously received—a bright boy of
fifteen acting as interpreter. He was the only
one who could speak English. They gave us
some exhibitions of their knowledge of Arithmetic and Geography; the former on a
black-board, the latter on a small globe. The
English speaking boy did most of it, and was
evidently the best scholar in school. He had
a fine head and brilliant eye. We requested
them to sing, but music was not in their
course of instruction.

In the evening, we returned to the ship.
Officers and men were busy all day Sunday, putting in freight. There was no public
religious service on board.

On Monday, we visited Amingo Island,
one of several lying in the bay. This one is
owned by the Steamship Company, and is
used as a burial ground. It is probably a
mile in circumference, covered with wood and
jungle, and rises abruptly some two hundred
feet. We saw nearly a hundred graves on the
steep hillside. Some were marked by marble

slabs, a few, by monuments, but most, with wooden head-boards.

Near the narrow foot-path, on a tree, was a large ants' nest. I had noticed them from the cars, as we crossed the Isthmus, but supposed they were excrescences belonging to the trees. Making a way to it through the nettles and briers, I found numerous covered ways leading up the trunk of the tree to the main nest, and again from the nest in all directions along the limbs and branches. Not an ant was visible. When I broke through one of the covered ways, there appeared scores of the little black workers, and instead of fleeing in terror, they rushed out to punish the invader. The material used in construction seems to be a dark vegetable matter, firmly cemented together, about as thick as light card paper, and nearly as strong. To see how their dwelling was constructed, knowing that they had plenty of time to repair damages, I punched a hole in their house. It was a conglomerate mass of irregular cells, apparently communicating with each other. A furious host rushed to the breach, and it was well for me that they had no wings. On another tree near by, was a nest larger than a bushel basket. Their building on trees may be necessary to protect them from the heavy rains that fall in these latitudes, and their covered ways are probably for the same purpose.

On the beach was another curiosity. On the shore at Panama, when the tide was out, we saw hundreds of active little crabs flying for refuge to the holes and crannies in the rocks. Here there were no rocks to hide in. On the beach, however, were plenty of empty shells lying scattered about. So every crab took refuge in a shell just large enough to admit his body. Nay, further, he would travel with it on his back, and make vastly better speed than a turtle. Nor did the large ones alone have a monopoly of this good sense, but little fellows, not larger than a bee or spider, would rush around in a shell not so large as a lady's thimble. I took up one of medium size, and intended to pull him out. Not by any means. He suffered himself to be torn asunder rather than yield.

Near the beach, in the crystal sea, was a magnificent jelly-fish, about a foot in diameter, and as beautiful in form as a flower. Our boatman took his oar and hoisted it upon the sand. It was at once a shapeless and disgusting mass. Like many other beautiful things in this world, they benefit us most the more we let them alone.

Returning to the ship, we rowed close past another island, hoping to have seen some monkeys. There are said to be a few in these islands, but we did not get a sight of any. As we returned to the ship the sun was intensely hot, though it was the twenty-third of December. The thermometer on board stood at 89°. Freight was still going in, and our ship was drawing twenty feet of water.

At 9 o'clock, next morning, the scows and lighters were cleared away, the anchor was weighed, a line was made fast to a buoy, our Chinese sailors tramped around the capstan singing their sailor song, the ship was headed round, the line thrown off, steam let on, the wheels revolved, and the "Constitution" was on her way toward the broad Pacific. To the right were some beautiful islands, on which were fine plantations—fields of bananas on the hill-side being visible a long distance. At noon we had made twenty-five miles and were in latitude 8°13' North—Course, West 4° South. In sight of land all day.

At night we had the first exhibition of fire-works at sea. The "phosphorescence," as it is usually called, behind the paddle-wheels and in our long wake, rivaled in splendor the milky way in the sky. To many of us the sight was wholly new. Coals mingled in water fail to convey the idea, because all our land experience shows that water immediately quenches them. Here, the more they were drowned and agitated, the more brilliantly they burned. The light made sometimes was sufficient to render newspaper type legible. Our wake was a highway of glory stretched out over the sea. The light is caused by myriads of little jelly-fish. Some think it due to phosphorus, others to electrical action in the body of the animal. Be the source what it may, it furnishes a charm for many long evenings on deck. One cannot help asking, whether John, the Revelator, had not looked upon such a scene, before he wrote of the "sea of glass mingled with fire."

Next day was Christmas. To one having always spent the day amid cold and snow, it seemed strange to pass it under a tropical sun, in summer garb, and glad to purchase ice for ten cents per pound. The day was spent pleasantly in conversation, reading, and various games. Interesting acquaintances had been formed long ere this, and the morning's wishes were as cordial as those in a family at home. The dinner, at five o'clock, was no ordinary affair. Even the sea furnished roast turkey and other good things in abundance.

In the evening, some young men got up an entertainment in the main saloon. A wild sky-lark from Washington, who had scarce seen a sober day after leaving New York, made a little speech on the character of the event we were celebrating, and then introduced the purser, who recited a selection from Hamlet; then followed a miserably sung solo, by the first speaker. The exhibition was witnessed, almost of necessity, by a large part of the cabin passengers. A whiskey punch came next. In disgust I went out on deck to look at the stars in the sky above, and at the fire in the deep below. Even the little jelly-fish were doing more than those men, in honor of Bethlehem's Star.

On Saturday, we were running along the coast of Guatimala, some twenty-five miles from shore. As the morning dawned, we got a good view of several inactive volcanos, one of which is known as the water volcano. It seemed impossible that they should be sixty or seventy miles away. Sheets of cloud, far below their tops, floated about them. Their relative positions changed very slowly, and when the evening's sun lighted up their summits, we seemed to be near them yet. The highest is about sixteen thousand feet high.

Having had an introduction to our captain,

3

at Panama, I found him not only the hardy and thorough sailor, but also a genial gentleman. He kindly gave me access to his maps, charts, and notes of former voyages. He was exceedingly desirous that I should conduct religious service the next day, and I was equally so to accept the invitation. But my vocal disability positively prevented. He said that the rules of the Company required him to conduct the service, or secure a substitute. For himself, he could not conscientiously, on one Sabbath, oversee the men putting in freight, when a rest would do all hands good, and then on the next, when no time would be lost, conduct religious services. He regarded it as a solemn mockery, and when there was no minister aboard he devolved the duty upon the purser. In regard to Sunday work in port, he was satisfied that the Company were losers in the end by requiring it. And in respect to all Sunday work, although not a professed Christian, he said he did not believe that man was "wise enough to cheat his Maker out of a day."

Next morning the Purser was sick. The captain again urged me to read service. I could not, but told him that I thought the duty was clearly his, under the circumstances. He had not done so for two years, and positively would not. However, when the hour arrived, the Purser crawled out of his berth and appeared in the main saloon, where the captain and twenty others were present for worship. Two-thirds of the passengers were absent. With much less effect than he had rendered Hamlet, he rushed through the formal Protestant Episcopal service, and closed within thirty minutes. The letter of the Steam Ship Company's law was complied with, and things moved on as usual.

In the afternoon, we were crossing the Gulf of Tehuantepec, and the sea was rough. We ran within twelve or fifteen miles of shore, for there is always here a stiff wind blowing down from the mountains of Mexico. Before evening, however, we were sailing in a sea as smooth as a vast meadow, and the sun went down amid piles of glory. The thermometer marked 89°,

and we retired with the promise that morning
would find us at Acapulco. And it did. The
thunder of our signal gun waked up everybody.
Looking out, I saw the dim outline of mountains
around us, heard the cable hum through the
hawse-hole, found it was two o'clock, and then
crept back to sleep a little more. At 4½
o'clock sleep was impossible. The natives by
scores had surrounded our vessel, in their
canoes. They carried torches, and made as
much noise as a fish market. Already they
were driving a lively trade with our passengers.
They had for sale, oranges, lemons, limes,
bananas, pine-apples, corals, various shells,
Panama hats, hammocks, parrots, paroquets,
turkeys, and chickens. A long cord and a
small basket or pail served to raise goods and
lower money. Their canoes were cut out of
a single mahogany tree, and the largest were
about three feet wide, and fifteen or eighteen
long. Most of them were much smaller. In
some were two men, in others, a man or woman
and boy, and a few were adroitly " manned " by
a single woman. One short paddle furnished

rowing apparatus. With all their noise they were exceedingly courteous to each other, and careful to avoid collision in managing their craft.

A company of nine of us got early "tea and toast" and went over to the city. A poor, miserable place it is. There are a number of stone and brick buildings, but most of the houses are built of poles and thatched with reeds or palm leaf. Streets wide, unpaved, irregular and ungraded. The only water-works seemed to be a public well, some eighteen feet in diameter, walled up about three feet above ground and uncovered. From this, women and boys were carrying water in three-gallon earthen jars, set upon their heads. On a rocky elevation the meat market was in progress. The meat was cut in long thin strips and hung over poles. It is so disposed of to keep it sweet. We visited the little Catholic Church. Its dirt and tinsel were about equal to what we had seen at Panama.

A half mile out, we visited a garden, or fruit farm. The cocoa palm, orange, lemon, lime, and tamarind trees mingled their shade, and pine-apples were growing in profusion. The signal gun warned us to return. As our boat went from the landing toward the ship, a youth of sixteen drove a lively trade swimming along and diving for dimes, which some of the passengers tossed far out into deep water. He brought each one up, held it up in triumph, and after a full breath, would call out, "catchee mo."

This little bay is a marvel of beauty, and so entirely surrounded by lofty hills and mountains, as at first sight, to one waking inside, to afford no egress. It is only about three-fourths of a mile in diameter; yet the water is deep, very clear, and a passage for the largest vessels is always open to the sea. From the ocean, too, it must have taken careful searching to find the entrance.

The discharge of sixty-five tons of freight was completed; anchor was weighed, and at 9½ o'clock we were under way again.

The coast of this part of Mexico presents no remarkable scenery—only a succession of low mountain ranges and hills. But the sea itself never lost interest. There is a weird witchery in waves.

The whole way from Panama, we had seen frequent specimens of snakes, about five feet long, swimming leisurely on the smooth surface of the sea. Then, too, there were smart looking turtles, about a half-yard in diameter, floating at ease. When the ship came near, they would duck their heads, paddle a little, and then presently look up at the receding monster with apparent satisfaction. Beside these on the surface, often far down in the clear depths, there were brilliant apparitions of beautiful fish. One, said to be a dolphin, looked like a section of rainbow in rapid flight. But there was something in the waves alone, more interesting than these. Their colors were as various as the colors of the sky, and their forms as different as the forms on land. Added to this was the interesting peculiarity, that while the changes in animal and vegetable forms and colors are so slow as not to be immediately noticed, here the transformation takes place under your eyes. The Atlantic had been cold as an iceberg, and as rough as a thunderstorm. Its waves were inky black and terrible. The Caribbean Sea was milder, by far, but yet gave evidence of being a near relative.

The Pacific was as different as peace is from war. Its colors were always milder. Even its larger waves, in the Gulf of Tehuantepec, seemed to be less angry, for on them were small secondary and tertiary waves, running another way, as if to soothe them. In the Atlantic, the secondary were like mounted furies urging the primary on. The Pacific had its immense, clean shaved meadows or prairies, with the flowers all beneath the surface. There seemed to be a cheerful spirit pervading and reigning over it. Sometimes, under the breath of that spirit, whole square leagues would smile into dimples. At night, our bow threw back this surface into folds of richest velvet, trimmed with lace, and sometimes sparkling with fire.

On Wednesday, January 1st, at five P. M.,

we dropped anchor in the harbor of Manzanillo. A mile above the entrance we saw a vessel at anchor, but our officers could not make her out. To our surprise and regret, we soon learned that it was the " Costa Rica," one of the Company's vessels, which had sailed from Panama twelve days ahead of us. She had got about eighty miles above Manzanillo, when her crank-pin broke. Having no duplicate, they set her meagre sails, and after great difficulty, and narrowly escaping wreck, they had worked her back to her present position. Her purser came in a boat and reported. Nothing remained but to take her passengers and baggage on board, and the ship, herself, in tow, for the remaining fifteen hundred miles. At nine o'clock, we steamed out toward her, but it was deemed unsafe to lay hold before morning.

With early dawn the transfer began, while our ship lay off and on near her. There were forty-five cabin passengers and fifty steerage. Some sublime grumbling followed, both on the part of recipients and received. Of course, nearly everybody preferred a state-room alone. I believe the fates "doubled up" those who grumbled most, for I had prepared to give a very cordial reception, to the unfortunate who should be assigned to me, and my preparation proved useless. Some of the transferred were as savage as bears. Two weeks extra on the Pacific had not pacified them, and one more rude than the rest, had a fracas with a waiter, the first time at table.

To get the vessel in tow was no small job. Though not more than a quarter of a mile from the rocky shore, she was anchored in fifty fathoms, both from stem and stern. Fearing that her bower anchor would not hold, and that she would swing upon the rocks, the captain had let go her kedge, which had become entangled, as we soon learned, in the cable of her bower. A twelve inch hawser was passed to her from our ship, and made fast. She attempted to weigh anchor. Link by link the donkey-engine lifted the ponderous chain, and after a long time, the huge iron knots came to the surface. A man was lowered to examine them; of course, he might as well have tried to "loose the bands of Orion."

Our ship was slowly swinging around into dangerous proximity, and our captain ordered them to "slip the cables and let go the anchors." There were high words and hard swearing on the "Costa Rica." They "could not get it loose!"

" *Cut* it then!"

That required time. To prevent collision, our vessel had to let them go, run out to sea, make a circuit and come up again.

It was two o'clock when the hawser was passed again, the cable was then cut, the anchors left, and the cripple was free to follow her leader. There seemed to be no end to "going slow," "steady" and "stopping." At 5 P. M., we had made twenty-five miles, passing some peculiar rocks known to be that distance from Manzanillo. A second hawser was then attached. Many stops and starts were made during the night, for the hawsers persisted in chafing, and something was frequently on the point of going wrong. It was a time of trial both to officers and men. Those Chinese sailors seemed as patient as oxen; and the waiters, too, all turned out, as occasion required, to haul those immense piles of twelve inch rope.

On Saturday, Jan. 4th, we crossed the Gulf of California, and at one o'clock on Sabbath morning, passed Cape St. Lucas.

At 10½ o'clock, the Purser again conducted service. With a splendid voice he rushed along at high speed, changing some words and riding over pauses without remorse. In a word, he "executed" it. He was very severe upon poor old Jacob.

The lesson included Gen. 50: 5, where he says to Joseph, "Lo, I die: in my grave which I have digged for me in the land of Canaan, there shalt thou bury me." He obliterated the colon after "die," and made the old man say, "Lo, I die in my grave which I have digged for me, &c." It was painful to hear a service, so profitable when devoutly read, reduced almost to comedy by the heartless coldness of the mere actor.

During the night of Jan. 7th, we arrived off San Diego. This is one of the regular stopping places, but having the "Costa Rica" in tow, and coal sufficient to reach San Francisco, they simply lay to, fired a gun and sent up rockets. A boat came off and exchanged despatches. Next morning we met the little steamer, "Gipsy," bound for San Diego. She slightly changed her course and stood for us. When she came within hailing distance, the following conversation passed:

Capt. Cavarly—"Do you want anything?"

Capt. of "Gipsy"—"No." "Have you any word to send to San Diego?"

Cavarly—"Tell them we are getting along well."

"*Gipsy*"—"All right."

Cavarly—"Had they heard the disaster to the 'Costa Rica?'"

"*Gipsy*"—"Yes, several days ago."

Hats were waved, steam was let on again, and soon the courteous little "Gipsy" was hidden behind its banner of black smoke, far on the horizon. We wondered how they had heard in San Francisco of the accident to the "Costa Rica," and were informed that a courier had been sent from Manzanillo to one of the interior towns of Mexico; that the despatch had been telegraphed thence to New Orleans, thence to New York, and thence to San Francisco.

We were now running within from ten to twenty miles of the shore, all the time. The summits of some of the mountains were lightly covered with snow. The thermometer had changed decidedly, reaching only 75° at midday, and we all had use for heavy clothing again. There were a good many invalids on board, and the great changes in temperature were very trying. When we left New York, the mercury was down to 23°. The steam pipes for heating the main saloon were all frozen up, and ice formed on the wash water in our state rooms. Overcoats and shawls were kept on at table in the evening, and piled upon the berths at night. Every degree

southward reduced the quantity, and at Aspinwall they had given place to the light summer
garb. Every day on the Isthmus an umbrella
was needed to protect the head from the burning sun. Now, as we approached San Francisco, the winter habiliments came forth again.

Below Point Conception we saw the first
mirage. It was very perfect. Though no
vessel was in sight upon the sea, yet off our
larboard bow was a schooner, with full sails,
apparently suspended in the air. Later in the
day, we saw the vessel itself by direct vision.

At noon, on Saturday, Jan. 11th, we passed
the Seal Rocks, the home of scores of seals.
We could see the huge fellows dragging themselves about, and faintly hear their mournful
bellowing.

Then the Golden Gate swung open before
us, the hills on either side rising five or six
hundred feet. They were treeless and shrub-
less, but just bursting into splendid verdure
under the influence of the winter rains.

Five miles through the channel, past two
frowning forts, and the broad bay was before

us with its islands, shipping, and adjacent city.

The "Costa Rica" was anchored, and by three o'clock the "Constitution" was made fast at her wharf. Thirty-one days and two hours from New York! Distance, 5,227 miles.

Happy are they who have the privilege of going to sea, and doubly happy they who stand on solid ground again.

When the voyage begins, a handkerchief, waved by the hand of a friend on the farthest point of the last pier, throws a ray of light that follows across several seas. When the vessel comes into the long desired port, friendly faces in the expectant throng shed light around, and make the voyager at once at home. So will it be when the voyage of life ends.

CHAPTER II.

WITH friends in San Francisco I spent five days. It rained nearly every night, but cleared in the morning. The thermometer reached 70° at noon, and did not fall below 45° at night. Grass was growing and flowers were blooming in the door-yards.

I had expected to find so young a place, like an over-grown youth—with very little solidity —but was thoroughly disappointed. While in some parts of the city there is abundant food for fires, the central and business portions equal the best of Chicago, Philadelphia, New York, or Boston. So wonderfully rapid has been the development from the passable to the comfortable, from the comfortable to the good, from the good to the better,

4

and from the better to the best, that even Chicago is outdone. Not only in manufactories, stores, banks, and hotels, are the best found, but also in schools, churches, libraries, water supply, pavements, street cars, police and fire departments, the people have taken advantage of what could be learned in older cities East, and in various respects have improved upon them.

The city government has some difficult questions with which to deal. Probably the most trying is the Chinese question. By treaty, China is open to Americans; by the same treaty, America is open to the Chinese. We go there by scores. They come here by thousands. San Francisco is their first stopping place. Whole squares are occupied by them alone. They have their stores, shops, saloons, theatre, and joss house or temple. From here they spread into every city, town, village, and nook in the State, and even across the mountains into eastern cities. Chicago, New York, Philadelphia, and Boston are already getting a sprinkling of them. They

SAN FRANCISCO TO VISALIA.

are called "heathen," and are said to be
depraved in morals.   Throughout the State, I
found a majority of the people complaining
bitterly of them.   They eat opium, gamble,
fight, and sometimes kill each other.   Americans, Spaniards, Irish and Germans do just
the same things, excepting that instead of
using opium they drink beer and whiskey.

The Chinese sailors and waiters on the
ship were the most orderly, obliging, patient, and faithful fellows that could be
found.   The only bad thing I knew the
waiters to be guilty of, was their inability to
say "curry and rice."   They persisted in calling it "cully and lice."   They are said to be
incurable thieves.   When nearing port, our
Steward had kindly warned me not to leave
any little articles lying about my state-room;
for, said he, "John will steal."   Contrary to advice, I risked them, and "John" took not even
a pin, though he had daily care of room and
contents.   From all I could learn, while in the
State, his chief crime seems to be, that he can
live on rice at a cost of about ten cents per

day, and thus save money, where an extravagant American starves.

I was in San Francisco, on a subsequent occasion, when the monthly steamer arrived from China. As usual, there were some hundreds on board. After being subjected to a rigid examination by the Custom House officers, they were taken by their friends, in large express wagons, toward the Chinese quarter. As they passed through one of the principal streets, the boys attacked them with stones, and some rushed up to the wagons, snatched articles out of their hands and bore them off in triumph. I saw another crowd following one who was carrying his own effects, in the usual way, in two large baskets slung at the ends of a short pole. The hoodlums seized hold of his baskets, swung them around, shoved him, jumped on his back, and finally threw him down on the pavement. Citizens stood and looked on, some blaming the boys, others cursing the long-cued Celestial. The "heathen" patiently bore it all, gathered himself up again, and quietly went on his way.

The boys were only doing what the majority
of the people approved, as expressed generally
in the secular and Roman Catholic papers.
While heathen christendom treats them thus,
the best Christian people look upon them as
men and brothers, whom it is our duty to treat
respectfully, and if possible convert from the
errors of their ancient superstitions. And
especially so, as they are brought to our shores
in our own ships. The Baptist, Presbyterian,
Congregational, and Methodist churches are
doing a good work in this direction. Rev.
Otis Gibson, of the Methodist church, has not
only nobly and strongly defended them against
the public storm, but he and his helpers are
leading some of them to Jesus.

I attended a service in the mission building,
at which there were present eleven women
and thirteen men, members of the church.
One of their number preached. His manner
was cool, earnest and dignified. All paid
strict attention. Mr. and Mrs. Gibson, with a
melodeon, aided the singing, and all joined in
heartily.

Though I could not understand the form of a single word, to feel the power required no human interpreter.

Later in the day, I attended a public service in the chapel further down the street. The door opens on a level with the pavement. Some would stop at the door, listen a few moments, and then pass on. Others slowly worked their way in, took seats, and heard the speaker through. The room was filled. Several native helpers delivered short addresses, and then Mr. Gibson spoke, also in Chinese, and closed the service.

While there are among them fearful evidences of vice, yet to one visiting their stores and shops as well as the missions and schools, it is evident that they are both as capable of conducting business and of being Christians as are the people of other nations. They are a wonderful people. With their light bronze complexion, almond eyes, long cues, curious dress, clumsy shoes, inexhaustible patience, genius in fancy work, heathen religion, infinite superstition, and vast numbers, they are a curiosity, a mystery, and a problem. To solve the problem " John," is a piece of work that will tax all the earthly wisdom of the State, and require all the divine influence of the Christian church.

On Monday, I attended the Methodist Preachers' meeting, at 711 Mission Street. In a little upper room, there were present eleven brethren. So small a number to supply so great a multitude, reminded one of the "five loaves and few small fishes;" but I thought of the time when there were only eleven at the foundation of the Christian Church. And these men were of the same Apostolic metal, with as warm hearts and as strong hands as had Peter, and James, and John. They gave reports from their respective charges, related personal experience, and considered the question of their "Sunday Law."

From San Francisco to Visalia is two hundred and thirty miles. By ferry, it is eight miles across the bay to Oakland. The bay itself is a magnificent sheet of water, about

forty miles long, with a maximum breadth of
twelve miles.   It would float all the navies of
all the nations.   Oakland is growing as rapidly as San Francisco.   For business, the latter
will naturally and necessarily forever hold the
first place.   It is Boston, New York, Philadelphia, Baltimore and Charleston all concentrated upon one spot.   But the former will
always be a preferable residence.   Its summer
comes in summer time, and as to winter, it
scarcely knows what it is.   At worst, it is an
April in the middle States.   The summer of
San Francisco is in midwinter.   Its summer
winds and sand storms are simply terrible, as
I found a few months later.   Furs and heavy
winter clothing are necessary on July after-
noons.   Unless so protected, those damp
ocean winds chill you to the very marrow.
In Oakland these are scarcely felt, their force
being expended before reaching the eastern
side of the bay.   Then, too, the city is embowered in shrubbery and shaded by a choice
profusion of fruit and ornamental trees.   Its
churches, schools, and handsome residences,

would lead a stranger to think it the growth of many decades, instead of a single score of years.

After running south-east several miles along the bay, the railroad turns eastward through Livermore Valley and Livermore Pass. Here were evidences of the strong and prevalent west winds. They sweep through this passage, as do waters through a mountain gorge. The trees, instead of growing up symmetrically, have their limbs mainly on the east side. Some, on exposed situations, resemble a flag-staff and flag in a stiff breeze.

Having left San Francisco, at 4 P. M., we reached Lathrop at eight. There we changed cars, turned southward and ran up the broad valley of the San Joaquin. We saw some fenced farms on the wide plain, and occasionally, by the light of the moon, could dimly distinguish the crest of the Sierra Nevadas, far to the east.

The night was cold. There was a stove and plenty of wood, but it was in such huge billets, that even the patience of the Chinese brakeman, could not prevail on it to burn. At four o'clock next morning, we had reached Goshen. In a half hour, the drowsy driver had harnessed up, and we commenced the short stage ride of seven miles to Visalia. The actual distance was greatly increased by the frequent mudholes into which we plunged, and the horrible corduroy over which we occasionally bounced.

Some of the passengers got sick. A stout sheep dealer thrust his head from the window, and paid a heavy tribute. My own recent experience at sea, now exempted me from further demands. A young Dutchman shut himself up like a jack-knife, lay on the front seat, and went to sleep. But he soon opened his blades, projected them in various directions for support, and then snored away again.

At six, the driver's shrill horn announced our arrival in town. A hot stove, and presently, a good warm breakfast at the Visalia House, effected an agreeable change. Later came a walk through town, and the presentation of letters of introduction.

This being the County seat of Tulare County, it is a centre of interest, for a large region around. The streets are unpaved, but wide, and cross each other at right angles. The stores and hotels are mostly substantial brick structures. The residences are generally frame, and many of them are models of taste and comfort combined. Some of the grounds are handsomely laid out, and flowers and fruit trees cluster about every dwelling. Through the centre of the town, flows a branch from the Kaneah River. It aids an engine in driving a mill, and affords abundant water for irrigation. There are four churches, Methodist Episcopal, Baptist, Presbyterian, and Methodist South. Though the membership is small in each, yet they are earnest and warm-hearted, and at various times I spent profitable hours with them in worship.

I remained here four weeks, boarding awhile at the hotel, and then with the excellent family of Mr. D. T. Atwell. For their oft repeated acts of kindness, to an invalid stranger in a strange land, they will not lose their reward.

Before I left Philadelphia, a friend had presented me a gun. In honor of his wife, I named it "Betsy." Thus far, by sea and land, she had been my companion, though as yet of no service. Here I began to *hunt*, for *health*. Hearing that small game was plenty, just outside of town, "Betsy" and I went out to explore.

Squirrels were said to be plenty, and in one of the first fields we found them; gray ground-squirrels! A half dozen scampered from the fence, ran to their mounds out in the open field, sat up upon their haunches, looked at "Betsy" and me, gave a little bark, and then popped into the adjoining holes. As I climbed into the field, a score started up from feeding in the low grass and grain. They seemed excessively wild, but I presently got within reasonable range, fired, and killed the first one. Then there was scampering over the whole field. To say there were hundreds would be within truthful limits. Examining my game, I found him to be about the same weight as our eastern gray squirrel, but with a much rougher

and duller coat, shorter body, and scarcely half
so much tail. They were wholly new to me,
and I believe, are confined to this coast.
Their numbers are so great and their voracity
so insatiable, that they devour whole fields of
grain, have been made a subject of State legis-
lation, and declared a nuisance. In the summer they get very fat, and when not too old,
are good eating.

The quail were abundant, but small and
hard to shoot. They kept well in the dense
brush, and as I was unpracticed on the wing,
I wasted no shot. I found afterward, that
there are two species of quail in the State, viz:
the ordinary, and the "Mountain" quail. The
last are a third larger than our partridge, and
have a beautiful black plume, about three
inches long, upon their heads. They are
found mainly in the foot-hills and mountains.
The former are a third smaller than our par-
tridges, and are not so handsomely marked,
but, what adds greatly to their beauty, they
also have a little black plume, about an inch
long. In the mountain quail, it is tapering

and floats backward; in the valley quail, the large round end is up, and it curves well forward.

The choicest game was the rabbits, or " cotton tails," as they are called there. They are about two-thirds the size of our eastern rabbit, very numerous and easily shot.

In skinning small game, I learned a new and interesting lesson. I never knew before, that they were dressed in "jacket" and "pantaloons," like other little folks. I always supposed that their skin was in one piece, and must be taken off by getting some one to hold the legs, and then tediously working the whole downward from the heels. When on one occasion "Betsy" and I had brought in four rabbits, Mrs. Atwell taught me otherwise. With the point of a knife she struck the division between the upper and nether garments in the middle of the back, inserted two fingers, pulled in opposite directions, and presto! there was the jacket, sleeves and all; there the pantaloons, legs and all; and there the divested game! The whole four were skinned in that many minutes.

Beside rabbits, there were plenty of hare.
They are familiarly called "jack rabbits," on
account of their long ears. They are nearly
twice as large as our rabbits, sometimes
reaching a weight of ten pounds. On one occasion I shot three, and their gravity induced
me to give two away before I got home.
They are splendid runners, and can keep out
of the way of the fleetest dog. When raised,
they will often run but a little way, and then
with ears erect, sit up upon their haunches,
and make observation. Where there are trees
or brush, it is then easy to creep up on them
and use shot. At long range, their heads are a
fine target for the rifle.

Two miles north of the town is a strong
branch of the Kaweah river, flowing westward
toward Tulare Lake, which is about twenty
miles distant. During most of the year, however, it is lost in the sandy plain before reaching the 'lake. On this stream, were a few
ducks. I succeeded in shooting one teal and
two mallard. There were said to be fish, too,
but a half day's honest effort on my part failed

to educe any evidence of the fact, either visible
or tangible. Not a bite. On another occasion, I tried them in a little slough on Mr.
Atwell's ranch. To dull my former disap-
pointment, I caught twenty-six. It must be
confessed, however, that they were not large.
Proudly carrying my scaly success back toward the town, I met old Capt. Bailey. He
jocosely asked me whether I was going "to
supply the hands on the new railroad." To
make a correct impression, many things have
to be weighed, or measured, as well as numbered. At Mr. Atwell's door hung a̅ spring
balance. The fish, with the osier upon which
they were strung, were hung upon it. The
index marked *one pound* and *three quarters!*
While in the State, I took care not to relate
that fish story to any Californian who was
capable of doing me an injury.

Large portions of the country about Visalia
are heavily wooded, mostly with black oak.
Some of the trees are evidently very old, and
north of the town I measured one of the

largest. It was a little over nineteen feet in circumference.

But the chief vegetable curiosity is the misletoe. It flourishes on several kinds of trees, but chiefly on the willow and cotton-wood, a tree slightly resembling our silver maple. This curious parasite sometimes appropriates the whole tree, growing out of every available limb and branch. Its branches, which are more like coarse vines than limbs, shoot out in great numbers at the same point, each again and again dividing into two. The leaf is small, thick, smooth, fleshy, and keeps yellowish green the whole year. It bears a fruit the size of a small pea. Each contains one seed covered with a glutinous substance. These are scattered from tree to tree by the birds, where they fix themselves to the bark, begin to grow, and tap the life forces of the tree. Many trees were in process of dying from its depredations, and many skeletons were standing, white, bony, and bare, as evidences of its power. In those cases, of course, the destroyer was also dead; but it was the last to die.

5

Like thieves, gamblers, rum sellers, and quacks, the parasites upon human society, they flourish wholly at the expense of the victim, and give up only when the victim is dead.

During this time there were frequent rains and considerable variation of temperature. On Monday, Jan. 20th, the thermometer at noon reached 75°. On the 21st, 70°. On the 29th, there was a stiff white frost, and the thermometer rose only to 58° at noon.

But while the water fell as rain at Visalia, it came down as snow upon the mountains and foot-hills, the nearest of which were twenty miles away. They seemed to be less than five. From the first foot-hills to the summit of the highest Sierra Nevadas it was said to be twenty or thirty miles more; and yet those snow-covered peaks, glistening in the sun, appeared to be within a few hours' walk. Those mountains are a sight of which one never wearies. The dusky outline in the early morning; the crest of fire when the sun first rises; the ever-green of the pine, and fir, and redwood, mingled with the snow; the abrupt cliff, the jagged edge, and the lofty pinnacle, with their shades and shadows, moving and changing with the journeying sun; in the evening, the fading out of those fine colors, and the swift change from burnished silver to dull marble, and from dull marble to bronze, and from bronze to iron—these are a daily exhibition worth more than any expressible money value.

I once timed the transformation from the moment I could last see the sun at Visalia. In a minute, the shadow struck the lowest foot-hills, then climbed from the lower to the higher hills, step by step, backward, upward, deepening the darkness in the already shady canyon, drawing a vail from ridge to ridge, enfolding evergreen and snow, pinnacle and cliff, steadily, visibly, until, in just twelve minutes, the last light lifted from the highest peak, and sombre night was seated on her ebon throne.

Looking at those mountains creates a desire to be among them. They are so great and noble, that you aspire to their company. I fortunately learned of a young man, five miles from town, who had a ranch up there, to which he intended going as soon as the snow sufficiently melted. An invalid, himself, he wished company. I went out to see him. The opportunity appeared to be what I wanted. I could work some for my board, and hunt as much as I wished. I agreed to go, purchased three heavy blankets, a few things necessary for camp-life, and packed my valise with food for "Betsy." Having two mouths of number eleven size, she was expected to be a liberal eater.

CHAPTER III.

WE set out at noon on February 11th. There were three of us: Mr. Swanson, whom all called "Doc," Burton, his brother, a boy of sixteen, and myself. We had one saddle-horse, and three hitched to a Jackson wagon, with high seat in front, mounted on springs. In the wagon were seventeen hundred pounds of freight, viz: wheat, barley, potatoes, a few articles of furniture and farming implements, sugar, coffee, tea, salt, soap, dried fruit, a little salt pork for a pinch when game might fail, a keg of syrup, blankets, plenty of heavy woolen clothing, Doc's old rifle, "Tom," "Betsy," plenty of ammunition, and a keg of whiskey. Doc was under medical treatment, and the last article was in his physician's prescription.

69

As we rolled out eastward, over the plain, on the south side of the Kaweah River, our road winding among the large oaks and cotton-woods, which in some places ventured to grow a mile from the water, the afternoon sun shone bright upon the green foot-hills and snow-covered mountains. There, before us, lay a mighty panorama of mountain masses, as various as you see the clouds in the sky, rising toward heaven more than two miles, and extending along the horizon a full hundred. Had they been carved out of ivory, and set with emerald, they could not have been more beautiful.

As we got through the heavy timber, and when the open plain spread before us, the hills seemed to recede. There were scattered trees and occasional houses and sheds of the ranchers. A little way from the road, some flocks of wild ducks swam upon a pond. Burton was riding the saddle-horse. I gave him "Betsy." He rode over, dismounted, crept along an old ditch, got into range, fired into a line of six, and soon came galloping after us, with five of the beautiful birds dangling to his saddle.

In the evening, we reached the foot hills, and put up at Duncan's ranch. Next morning, Mr. Duncan, with two extra horses, helped us up the first hill. There was as good driving and pulling done as I ever saw. Up, upward, and still upward, hill upon hill. I never before realized the wealth of the upper world in unlimited sky room. By noon, we had made six miles. We left seven hundred pounds of freight at Jordan's, made four miles more, and put up at Carter's ranch. We were about three thousand feet above tide.

In the morning, there were strong indications of rain. Heavy masses of cloud hung upon the surrounding mountain tops. We set out, however, and soon reached a hill, that in any other place would be called a mountain. Before we reached the top, the mist and rain had turned to snow. Covered with my gum blanket, I rode ahead with the shovel, to try the dangerous places and repair the road. At eleven o'clock, we reached the cabin of Mr.

Cahoon, a hunter, where we received a hearty welcome, gathered around a rousing fire, and had for dinner, plenty of fried venison, good bread and hominy. That was one of the brightest fires and best dinners I ever enjoyed. The snow covered the ground, and we stopped for the night. Rumbo, our good dog, entertained himself handsomely on the numerous deer carcasses that lay about the cabin.

Next day the sun shone. We had yet four miles, over the Black Hill and down into Grouse Valley, and we were at our journey's end. Before it was reached, however, we had to drag through snow a foot deep. In the valley there was none. We got there about noon. The cabin was twelve feet square, roofed and sided with clap-boards, split from a pine log, having a wavy grain. Hence, while the protection from rain was complete, there were numerous and ample cracks for ventilation. A stone fire-place and chimney, at one side, served at once for fire to cook our victuals and to warm the house. We had plenty of plain food, a good supply of cooking utensils, considerable skill in their use, a breakfast table with falling leaves and oil-cloth cover, and appetites to clear it of any reasonable amount that came upon it.

Bunks three feet wide, and two feet from the ground, with their clap-board bottoms, were our beds. Upon the boards a bear skin, upon that a straw tick, and then all the blankets you had. You sandwiched yourself between them, higher up or lower down, according to the varying temperature. With no garret, no up stairs, no cellar, no floor and no ceiling, the trouble of house cleaning was reduced to a minimum. A daily application of the broom to the earth, was the extent of the necessity. With such simple surroundings, the happy occupant is more than a match for an impertinent "Bridget."

The valley is a gem of beauty, about four thousand feet above the sea, containing probably five hundred acres of tillable land, several thousand of good stock range, and is surrounded by mountains from one to two thousand feet high. Some of these are covered with oak, manzanita, and chaparral; others with pine, cedar, and fir. Some excellent springs furnish abundant water. There were no trout in the streams, and I thought it was no wonder they had not yet got up there, if the Mosaic Chronology is correct.

Quail were abundant, a few rabbits and hare, plenty of foxes and wild cats, squirrels and grouse high up among the pines, an occasional panther, and a good many deer. Owing to the scarcity of acorns, the bears had withdrawn southward, the previous fall.

We got into the valley on Friday, February 14th. On Saturday morning, the thermometer was down to 34°. On Sunday afternoon, it began to snow and blow. The mercury fell to 32°. At 7, P. M., the snow was five inches deep. We got in wood and prepared for a rough night. The snow drifted in and sprinkled floor and bunks. It looked unhealthy for invalids. At six, next morning, the thermometer marked 23°. The snow was eight inches deep. An inch of ice covered the water in our pail on the table, and all the potatoes in the sack, at the head of my bunk, were frozen solid. But it cleared off beautifully. We were in the midst of the ivory splendor visible from Visalia. Well booted, I took "Betsy," and made a successful attack upon the quail. At noon, the thermometer rose to 49°.

Mr. Cahoon, the hunter, had given me an invitation to come down and go with him on a hunt.

The low temperature and deep snow, up there, confirmed me in the belief that I had better accept.

I walked down on Wednesday afternoon, and fortunately for me, a stray horse had broken the trail through the foot and half of snow that lay on the intervening mountain. Mr. Cahoon came in, having killed two deer. Next morning, he brought them home, and in the afternoon, I went with him to follow three others, whose tracks he had seen near camp. There was no snow, excepting two or three inches on shaded north hill sides, Cahoon's being about a thousand feet lower than Grouse Valley.

It was exciting business, especially as we crept through the chaparral, where we found on the brush, that raked our own backs, the hair fresh from theirs. It is amazing what low, narrow places they could go through! The best we could sometimes do was to lay our guns on the ground, turn quadruped of the Saurian genus, and worm through after them. Thus, over hills, down into ravines, around steep hill sides, on and on, three miles. Still they were ahead of us, and out of sight.

A fresh deer track gathers about it much of interest. In itself, it is beautiful. The delicate point of the toe, the graceful curve of the side and heel, indicate the work of an artist. As the beautiful curves in the form of a capital letter, made by a skillful penman, are readily known not to be the work of a heavy handed writer, so the track of a deer is easily distinguished from that of a pig or sheep. You know it to be the track of an animal which, though it has no wings, yet royally disdains the ground upon which it treads. Then, too, a fresh track means a live deer not far off. In a moment, you may be upon him. And to kill a deer, a real live deer in the woods! A cart load of quail, or a boat load of ducks is poor in comparison. Further, to a hungry hunter, it means meat. To him, "meat is the staff of life." And closely associated with those tracks are shoulders, and hams, and sirloin! His gun gets impatient, his knife is hot and bloody. In imagination a tender-loin hisses upon the coals! Like Job's horse, "he smelleth the battle from afar." But very unlike Job's horse, I got exceedingly tired and returned to camp. Mr. Cahoon went a mile further, and gave up the chase.

Next day, while he prepared grub for a five or six days' hunt, I went down to the Kaweah, at the nearest point, and saw many tracks, but no game. I could doubtless have killed several deer had they only stood long enough in those tracks! Returning up that fearful hill, I counted the paces from the river to camp—four thousand nine hundred and forty:

rising in the two miles and two hours about one thousand nine hundred feet.

At 7.50, on Saturday morning, we set out for the lower foot-hills along the Kaweah. As this was an average expedition, and really my first good lesson in hunting, I will give some details. Cahoon's rifle was a three-barrelled revolver; the three cast-steel barrels being put together in the form of a triangle, and having one lock. It carried seventy round, or thirty-five minie balls to the pound. He almost invariably used the minie.

Not expecting to go on a long hunt, I had brought down only fourteen rounds of buck shot and ball. I told him I thought it was not enough for *six days*. His reply I shall never forget—"If you have good luck, it's plenty, if not, it's too much."

We had five horses, two under saddle and three with packs. The bell, on old "Sallie," the bell-mare, was muffled. Her yearling colt, "Kitty," sported from side to side along the trail. Mr. Cahoon led the van, the three pack-horses followed, and I brought up the

rear. It was a bright morning, and as we descended toward the river, the snow wholly disappeared. The leaves were out on the buck-
eye bushes, the grass and wild flowers were
peeping through the pulverized granite soil,
and far below us, through the principal canyon,
among the live oaks and boulders, the river
wound its way westward and downward toward the plain.

By the morning breeze, already setting in
from the west, the music it made was borne
even up to us, and far over the hills. Most of
the trail was good, some of it poor enough,
and a small portion miserably bad. Indeed,
in some places, there was none at all.

We dismounted, led our saddle-horses, and
had to drive the trembling pack-brutes over
some slippery rocks.

Passing through a flat, among large timber
and brush, Cahoon suddenly dropped his
lead-rope, ran forward, raised his gun, lowered
it, ran around a clump of brush, and presently
returned, saying, "I ought to be kicked, for not
killing that deer!"

Being at the rear of our little caravan, I had not even seen it. But now our march became exciting. Down another mountain side, through another flat, and he repeated the movement. This time, he advanced further behind the brush. Bang! bang! bang! While the triple report was reverberating among the mountains, I reined up, tied my horse and the old bell-mare, threw off my coat, and ran forward with "Betsy" to see the battle. A deer, with its hind leg broken, was running up over a high rocky ridge. Thinking my capacity equal to the capture of a cripple, I started in pursuit, while Cahoon was reloading. Passing around a clump of chaparral I heard a rustle and saw a line of bushes shaking, and then away below, a bounding deer emerged, crossed the brook, and sped up the opposite hill-side, pausing to look round when three hundred yards away, then off to the mountain.

Cahoon had shot one dead, and after reloading, followed an uninjured one around the hill side.. When I reached the summit, in

pursuit of the wounded one, his gun roared
again. Looking down, I saw another jumping
around with both fore-legs shot off. When he
had cut its throat, he, too, came to hunt the
track of the wounded one. We got separated.
I found the track first, and followed it down the
hill a half mile to the river bed. There it
seemed to disappear, but after a long search,
I found the track and a puddle of blood among
the sand and boulders. Sure of soon finding
and killing the poor beast, I pursued. The
boulders rattled. I looked up, and there it ran,
eighty yards away, and was instantly behind
a bank. It was soon in a perfect jungle of
brush, briers, and live oaks. I followed with
care, and heard it three times, but it always
kept out of sight. Passing out to clear ground,
I went around and beyond to head it off;
returning through the thicket I missed it, and
getting back to my former track, I saw the
nail-print of Cahoon's shoe. He was now in
ahead of me. In a minute I heard the report
of his rifle, went out again to clear ground,
followed him toward the base of the hill, and

6

was in time to see him cut its throat. He had shot it through the back, as it ran, at about one hundred and fifty yards. Having taken out the entrails and cut off the head, he hung it by the neck on a tree, about three feet clear of the ground. We then went back and treated the other two in the same way, returned to our horses, went two miles further down the river, forded it, and took possession of a deserted shepherd's cabin, on the north bank. It was 3 o'clock. We prepared and enjoyed a hearty dinner. Cahoon took the horses a mile and a half up a side canyon, hobbled two, left them, and looked for game. I fixed up the cabin, prepared wood, rigged my fishing tackle and tried the fish. Night came, Cahoon returned gameless, and I without so much as a nibble.

The night was beautiful, and in the music made by the river, there was a witchery that charmed me for hours. The bed of the Kaweah is exceedingly rough, and the descent toward the plain very rapid. Analyzing the noise made by the rushing waters, though it was not loud, yet in it I could detect all the sounds I had ever heard: the roar of distant thunder, the boom of artillery, the blast of the bugle, the shrill note of the fife, the roll of the drum, the clang of the gong, the ringing of bells, the full tones of the organ, the twitter of birds, the scream of wild beasts, the melody of sacred music, the vocal gymnastics of the opera, the solemn wail of the winds among the mountain pines, and the confused noises of the city. I had heard the music of other streams, the thunder of Niagara, the dash and roar of the ocean in a storm, both far from land and on the beach and rock-bound coast, but none of them equaled in variety those night sounds of the Kaweah. It was God's orchestra among the mountains.

Sabbath morning came bright. Cahoon put up a lunch and went hunting. I got a horse and went four miles down the river, to Duncan's ranch, for my mail. There was no religious service within reach; but the letters I received, from loved ones far away, were as long as a sermon ought to be, and to me, much more refreshing than many I have read. "As cold waters to a thirsty soul, so is good news from a far country."

As ought to be expected from Sunday hunting, Cahoon returned in the evening, without game. He had seen some signs of deer, but thought we were too far down, and concluded to return a few miles in the morning.

Monday came, and with it clouds and rain. However, we packed up and went back, near where he had killed the deer on Saturday. Here there is a wide flat, and the north and south forks of the Kaweah unite. A deserted adobe house stood just below the fork. The doors and windows were boarded up and secured with ropes and nails. The heavy storm-clouds were trailing white robes of snow over the surrounding mountain tops. Just as we reached the adobe, they came down upon us in torrents of rain. A knife and a moment served Cahoon to sever a rope, push back an old table, and prostrate a rude door. We were at once under roof and obligation to the builder. A plank floor, an old table, and a fireplace were the luxuries of the inside. The earthquakes had cracked and thrown the walls out of plumb, yet it served our purpose better than a palace. The horses were turned loose to graze. We unpacked our boxes, and prepared to make ourselves at home.

To those fond of minutiæ, the contents of our packs would be of interest. As trifles are the most of life, and always necessary to complete a picture, I will empty them out. Here are the contents: seven loaves of graham bread, one corn bread, some choice slices of venison, and a can of venison tallow in which to fry them; frying pan, half peck of potatoes, three quarts cooked hominy, small box each of tea, pepper, and salt. Coffee pot and small bag of ground coffee. An axe, two iron spoons, whetstone, spring balance, gun fixtures and ammunition, towels and soap. Knives we carried. For plates we used pieces of bread, and saved washing by eating them. Over the rawhide boxes containing these things, were tied a tent and two large bear skins. Our blankets were under the saddles. Thus we were in want of no necessaries, and for luxuries we had no use.

In the afternoon it cleared. We went out to hunt. Cahoon killed another deer. I did not see even a track.

On Tuesday, we took a lunch, crossed the south fork, and went up into the mountains. I found a fresh track, and followed it a long distance, got up among the snow-clouds, and saw how snow and rain are made, but saw no game. I got also among the poison oak, "rhus toxicodendron," not yet knowing which shrub was it. I learned, however, for it poisoned me severely. To add to my discomfort, my boots ran crooked, travelling along the oozey hill-sides. While wearily trudging toward camp, I saw a lone wild pigeon, fired at it a load of buck-shot and missed it. Tired and hungry, I got back to camp at five o'clock, and concluded that hunting for health in that kind of style would not likely prove successful. A half-hour later, Cahoon came in, having fired at deer thirteen times and killed one. The mist and rain obstructed the sights on his rifle.

On Wednesday, I tried the fish again, **and** caught one poor little sucker. Then the quail —"Betsy" was at home among them. Cahoon killed another deer. On Thursday, I hunted for health about camp, by chopping down an oak. There was an abundance of red-wood brought down by the flood, but it popped so badly that we could not safely use it. It persisted in firing the floor by day, and burning holes in our blankets at night. Cahoon crossed the north fork, and returned by $3\frac{1}{2}$ o'clock, with four deer. He had seen nineteen. In the evening he packed in the others, and skinned out and cut up six of the ten. There is no division between the jacket and pantaloons of a deer. He took them off in one piece, but so quickly, that it reminded me of Mrs. Atwell skinning the rabbits. On Friday morning, we packed up. Our bread, potatoes and hominy were gone; but the ten deer made a load for the three pack-horses. We got back to the cabin at two o'clock. Though luckless myself, I had seen how it was done, and knew thoroughly how *not* to do it.

I saw that hunting was an art, and that it required, in its practice, more muscle and better boots than I was possessed of. I had learned also to know that detestable shrub, "poison oak." Until I got relief, by using a solution of borax, I patiently scratched my burning skin, and quietly anathematized both root and branch of the miserable vegetable. To aggravate the annoyance, Mr. Cahoon handled it with impunity, and the horse I rode would steal two steps out of the trail to nip it. A month later, there was a severe frost, and my heart was made glad by seeing its brilliant green leaves turn black and die. It may be good as a medicine, but it is far from agreeable in general application.

When I got back to Grouse Valley the snow had disappeared, and we went to work clearing and plowing ground. I took hold of the mattock and developed muscle, grubbing wild cherry and wild plum bushes. We plowed about six acres, and sowed with wheat and barley. To protect from stock, we then built a fence around about twelve acres. This, with intervals of hunting, reading and writing, washing and mending (it took a good deal of both), filled pleasantly up the next six weeks.

During this time, there was another phase of hunting for health, that would not be recommended by medical men. Rumbo was fond of treeing foxes and wild cats. The former running up a tree, was to me a matter of curiosity. This "treeing" never occurred by day, but at all hours of the night, at various distances from camp, and generally in very rough places. But sleep forsook my eyes and slumber my eyelids, whenever I heard Rumbo bark. Several times, between the hours of eleven and two, I got up, took "Betsy," a piece of candle, matches, and a thin bundle of long pine splints for a torch, and tramped a devious way over hill, across ravine, among rocks and brush, sometimes compelled to creep upon hands and knees, beneath the chaparral. To find the baying dog and the tree was comparatively easy. Sometimes equally so, to see and shoot the fox. But it often happened that the tree was a thick live-oak, and oftener, that the fox had gone. He would run up the trunk, slip far out on a horizontal limb, jump off and leave the dog behind, "barking up the wrong tree." Sometimes they would run down, on seeing me approach, and get safely away both from dog and gun. When the tree was large, I often had to build a fire and search long, mostly in vain. Once, after a careful and protracted search, I saw the beast only twenty feet above me, with his head resting in a fork, and his eyes fixed steadily upon me. The wonder was, that I had not seen him sooner. As the roaring fire flashed up, I could see his ears, his nose, his eyes, and the fine dark lines across his visage. It seemed a pity to spoil so pretty a face. But his skin was what I wanted, and all but his head would be uninjured. I took good aim, and planted a load of shot right in his head. There was a rustle among the leaves, a rattle against the limbs, and a thump upon the ground.

But the dog did not pick it up and shake it, as was his vigorous custom. Going to investigate the cause, I found it. It was dead as a block. And it was a *block!*—the stump of a broken limb. I had made a good shot.

On another occasion, I shot the beast by starlight. When the dog had finished his shake, I picked up the animal, and it proved to be a wild cat. It was a fine specimen. I dressed and lined the skin for a rug. It was a beauty. The fox-skins afterward went through a similar process. They are handsome, too, but being unacquainted with the business, I failed to save their magnificent tails.

About the middle of March, as I returned from Visalia, where I went for my mail every two or three weeks, I saw a fine lot of suckers in a creek, near the Kaweah. I dismounted, and rigged a large hook with six inches of line, to the end of a ten foot rod. From a high bank above, I carefully lowered it among them. Two shepherds came by, stopped to see the sport, and expressed a doubt about any plan but the spear. I replied that the spear was barbarous, and that I had hooked them so, cast. In twenty minutes, ten of them were floundering in the sand. I strung upon a willow, and hung them upon the horn of my saddle. The ten weighed seventeen pounds.

At this time the thermometer ranged from 35° to 45° at six A. M., and from 60° to 75° at noon.

Having received a cordial invitation from Mr. Cahoon to live with him, and teach him to write, I concluded to make the change. There was too much hard work on the ranch. Though what I did, beyond the worth of my "grub," was wholly voluntary, yet I could not be idle with work around crying to be done. And even to earn my board was a serious matter. For while my digestion appeared to be equal to any task, my muscle was not on a par with the requirements of the mattock and axe.

CHAPTER IV.

ON April 5th, I packed up and went down to Cahoon's. His cabin was built of heavy oak posts set on end, blocked and plastered with clay. It was twelve by sixteen feet, with chimney and fire-place at one end. It was well roofed with clap-boards, and for a floor had plain mother earth. There were three bunks, two single ones, and one large double one. The latter, we used for a sideboard. Our table was an humble affair, but a blessing was as devoutly asked, and the food as heartily devoured, as at the best walnut extension. It was an inverted store-box, about two by three feet.

Before Mr. Cahoon commenced dressing his deer skins, of which he had one hundred and twenty, we went on a fishing excursion to the Kaweah. From 8½, A. M. until 2, P. M., we travelled and fished. As usual, Cahoon had all the luck. But in this case, not much to be elated over—one speckled trout of about three-quarters pound weight! We could not imagine what had become of "the other one." Failing to find it, after several hours vigorous search, we concluded that it must have met with an accident among those fearful boulders.

There were here, in the mountains, only a few miles distant, both a Mr. Hector and a Mr. Homer. They were distant relations of the ancient worthies of classic renown. By agreement, the latter came to our camp, one evening, to accompany Mr. Cahoon on a hunt the next day. An evening around a good fire with these old mountaineers is a luxury. Mr. Homer could neither play a harp (though I dare say he would help string up a liar), nor could he dash off the Greek hexameters. What was more important, on the present occasion, he had a good memory, and was capital on a story. One or two will bear repeating;

and his gray hairs, in connection with internal evidence, left no doubt upon our minds as to their truth.

He told of a gentleman, down in Kern County, who always carried a sheath-knife, and he explained why: once, when passing along a narrow trail in the coast range, quick as lightning from the cloud, he was crushed to the ground. In a moment he was aware of the situation. From an overhanging tree, a panther, watching for deer, had leaped upon him, fixing its teeth into his right shoulder, and its hinder claws upon his thighs. It seemed in a fair way to make venison of *him*. His face was to the earth, and he could scarce move. His gun lay useless at his side. Fortunately, on this occasion, in a sheath at his breast, he had a knife, which he seldom carried. Struggling quietly, he by and by got hold of the handle, writhed partly around, locked the hind legs of the beast with his own, got the point of the knife about where he thought it ought to be, and with his left hand gave it a quick and terrible plunge. The beast let go its hold, but *he* now held on. It struggled, rolled over, and died. He had thrust it through the heart. His heavy coat and under clothing had prevented serious wounds. Ever afterward he carried a sheath-knife, and when on a wooded trail, kept an eye upward, too.

Of this same man, Mr. H. related the following "bear story:"

Near their camp, in the Sierra Nevadas, two men at different times, on a certain trail, had recently been chased a long distance by a large bear. As it was late in the evening, they could not say whether it was a "brown" or a "grizzly," but he was a huge fellow at any rate. This gentleman on returning, one evening, passed another camp, five miles from his own, and had to take this same trail. He was on horseback, and carried a double-barreled shotgun, well charged. Of course, he thought about that bear. Night had already set in. It was foggy, and the ground was muddy from recent rain. He had passed the camp but a little way, when he thought he heard footsteps in the trail behind him. Putting spurs to

his horse, he concluded that he would prudent-
ly leave it behind, whatever it might be.
Slacking speed, by and by, he took it more
leisurely, thinking he had possibly been mis-
taken, at any rate. But presently, slap! slap!
slap! in the mud, he certainly hears the foot-
fall of the beast pursuing him. Again he put
spurs to his horse, and the poor brute thundered
over the rocks, rushed down awful steeps, and
smoked as he toiled up the rugged passes.
Another mile made, another pause in speed.
Surely he had now left it far behind. But no.
In a few minutes, that now terrible foot-fall
strikes his ear again. It is nearly three miles
to camp. Again he tries to leave his dreadful
pursuer behind, and dashes through the gloom
another mile. Things had now come to a
crisis. His horse was ready to give out. But
he had a loaded gun. Why not make a stand,
like a man, and use it? He resolved to do so;
or, at least, give it the contents of his gun, and
then leave as fast as his horse might be able.
Reining up in the trail, but leaving the
horse's head toward camp, he turned half

7

round in the saddle, summoned all his courage, and waited. But not long. Slap! slap! slap! came those tremendous paws, making melancholy music in the mud. With the gun to his face, he peered back into the darkness, and when at a few steps distance the monster's form appeared, he pulled both triggers, turned in his saddle, clapped spurs to his horse, galloped the remaining mile, and in sweat and terror tumbled into camp. His camp fellows were amazed. However, it was thought best not to return until day-light would reveal the kind of animal they had to deal with. Early dawn found them cautiously approaching the spot. And lo! there it lay. He had shot it fair in the head, and had carried away one lobe of the brain. It was a big, brown—*mule!*

Daylight had brought trouble to the neighboring camp, too.

A man was spending the night there, and had picketed his beast to feed. It had got loose, had seen the horse pass, and, donkey like, had followed after. For its unwavering affection for the horse, it had lost its brains.

The owner missed, tracked, and found it. The murderer, too, was found, plead guilty, and asked the value of the mule. Sixty dollars. They were both generous, split the difference, and J. P. L. paid thirty dollars for his dead shot.

But to return to our own narrative. Next morning, they went hunting, not for pleasure, but for meat. We were out. At 3½ P. M., they came back, without having even seen game, though they had ridden twelve miles and walked six. Like a good minister, who was once greatly comforted by listening to the evident failure of a prominent pulpit orator, so was I, that old hunters could sometimes "get into the brush," and come out with nothing more than scratches.

The weather, during April and May, was charming. The last frost, an unusually late one, had occurred on the 7th of April. The hills were clothed with green, and the plains below were carpeted with flowers. By the last of May, the flowery carpet had crept up, like a sunrise reversed, and reached our camp. Before starting to Visalia, one day, I gathered, for an amateur botanist in town, twenty-three varieties of wild flowers, that grew within rifle-shot of our cabin.

The good old robin sang his morning and evening song, and quails in abundance whistled about our camp. At night, the foxes barked, and as we had no dog, they came and went unmolested.

Our stock of literature was not large, but very select. While we were beyond and above the influences of the Daily Press, we had "The Christian Advocate," an occasional "Harper's Monthly," the "Overland Monthly," "The Bible," and "Thompson's Lectures."

There was no church nearer than about twenty-five miles. But on Saturday evening, or early on Sabbath morning, we washed up and put on clean clothes, like civilized people. Mr. Cahoon omitted his usual work on Sunday, and I spent most of the day in reading. A half mile east of our cabin was a grand Sabbath resort. It was the summit of a hill, overlooking several miles of the noisy Kaweah, which was two thousand feet below. Around were rocks, and trees, and birds. The fox and the wild cat had hidden way. The panther lay coiled in his lair. The timid deer suspiciously snuffed the air, or quietly grazed on the grassy slope.

Beyond, and rising in majesty above the river and dark, deep canyons, were the lofty heights of the Sierras. Robed in snow and mantled with cloud, their feet upon the foundations of the earth, and their heads amid the heavens, they stood preaching the power and wisdom of their Maker.

To the auditor was announced the text, "Day unto day uttereth speech," and if he were not both deaf and blind, he could both hear and see the sermon. The crystal Kaweah struck music from a granite instrument of many octaves, and the breath of the Almighty bore it sweetly and powerfully up to the summit of the hills.

What a lavish expenditure of divine excellence among these mountains! The ordinary grove and choral music of the camp meeting are feeble in comparison. The devout, human soul could readily join the seraphim, whom Isaiah saw, and cry, "Holy, holy, holy, is the Lord of hosts; the whole earth is full of his glory."

The poet has said:

> "Full many a gem of purest ray serene,
>   The deep unfathomed caves of ocean bear—
> Full many a flower is born to blush unseen,
>   And waste its sweetness on the desert air."

This is only a hint at the whole truth. From the little we know, it is likely that those unseen gems and flowers are not simply "full many," but vastly exceeding in abundance those already known. Humanity, cursed so deeply by sin, and expelled from Eden, is feeding upon the meagre fruit that falls from the boughs of a few trees that over-hang the hedge surrounding God's infinite garden.

But this is a practical world. A Sabbath soon ends. "Six days shalt thou labor." We soon descend from the sanctuary to food and raiment; and unless the God who dwells in the sanctuary, abides in our hearts, life is poor and hard indeed. With him dwelling

there, it becomes a blessing to man and an
honor to his Creator.

To return to daily employments. We kept
two gentle cows. At night, they were put
into the corral, and their calves were allowed
to race around and nip the fresh grass. By day,
they were pent up, and the cows allowed to
roam at large. I enjoyed milking them; and
still more, drinking the milk. But after darning
socks, the most interesting domestic employment was, washing our tin dishes. I know it
is generally regarded as a menial, tiresome,
unprofitable and despicable employment.
With plenty of hot water and soap, I enjoyed
it. To be an *agent* in a *cleansing* process is
no mean business.

I consider it vastly more dignified and
worthy of the divine nature of man, to wash
a plate, or sweep a street, than to injure the
health and pollute the air by smoking tobacco.
In many employments you toil long and hard,
without making your mark. A good dish
washer never does. "But it has to be done
over, and over, and over again." So does

eating, so does sleeping, so does plowing, and so does preaching. The most noble acts beneficently allow repetition. The worst, ought never to be done at all.

When on a trip down the valley, about the last of April, I had a chase after the Sand-hill Cranes. They come down upon the plains in great numbers, to feed upon the grass-hoppers. They descend from an immense height, often two miles or more. You can hear their plaintive cry before they are visible. Presently, after earnest search, you see a number of little dark discs circling round and round, and slowly enlarging. In a half-hour, they settle upon the plain, form a long line, and sweep the "hoppers" clean. As they were said to be excellent eating, and not having "Betsy" along, I borrowed an old shot-gun, mounted my horse and rode out toward them. Their sentinels, posted on prominent places, gave ample warning, and flock after flock arose before I got within a hundred yards. Had they known how little was the impending danger, they might have let me come much nearer. I finally fired into a flock as they rose, but they all went on their way singing. If there was any satisfaction, in not having made any poor cripples, I had it. They are occasionally killed with the rifle, but very seldom with shot.

Early in May, it got quite warm. On the fifth, the thermometer at 6, A. M., marked 52°, at noon, 80°.

The rattle-snakes came out. Several were killed near us. I had never heard the rattle, and there possessed me an indefinable fear of meeting the first one. On the sixth, returning from a hunt, I was walking along a narrow trail, when just beside me, in grass six inches high, I heard the terrible rattle. I stepped back, and looked for the snake; for though the language was new, an idiot would need no interpreter. Not being able to see it, I advanced again. It reared its head, rattled violently, threw its neck into a horizontal spiral, fixed its villianous eyes upon me, darted out its tongue, and looked the very personification of mischief. Not liking his looks, and having had enough of his music, I improved his visage with a load of buck-shot, and captured his instrument.   It had seven rattles.

The boys, on a neighboring ranch, killed over thirty in one season. But they seldom bite either man or beast, as in almost every case they give warning, and both man and beast hear and speedily heed it. The horses seem to dread them more than men do.

In the lower foot-hills, about the last of May, a man was bitten by one. He had gone down to a little spring to get a drink. Having no cup, he put down his hand, when, without touch and without warning, he was struck. He went twenty miles to Visalia for medical aid, suffered intensely for two days, gave up hope of recovery, but finally got well.

Mr. Cahoon, once, went down to a spring for a drink, and right at his feet lay coiled one of the venomous reptiles.   Standing still, and holding his rifle within a few inches of its head, he fired. The snake lost its head, and he burst his gun. Being so near the ground, the barrel split from the muzzle back six inches.

Beside rattle-snakes, there were very few

dangerous beasts of any kind.   I saw but one
centipede, one scorpion, and two tarantulas,
while in the State.   I found and captured one
"Mason Spider."   I was crossing a ditch, just
below our cabin, when, in the bare, sloping
bank before my eyes, his little door popped
shut.   I watched for him often, but never saw
the door open again.   Some weeks afterward,
I carved him out.   The earth was very hard;
so with a knife I worked all away, but a small
pillar containing his den.   The upper part of
this I fit into a little tin can, got him into it,
packed him up and brought him home.   He
did not survive the confinement.   When unpacked, six months later, only his bones lay
at the bottom of his silk-lined house.   The
door is curiously hung.   The hinge needs no
oil, and it never creaks.

There were lizzards by the score and thousands.   At first I dreaded them, but soon
I became accustomed to the half dozen or
more that scampered about our cabin.   Their
beautiful colors, active movements, and skill
in catching flies, rendered them interesting

companions.   One ran over my head as I lay
in my bunk.   Their rapidity of motion is
wonderful.

During May, I had some interesting excursions to the lower Kaweah, after the white
trout.   They come up from Tulare Lake, and
are no mean fish.   In weight, they range the
whole way up to ten pounds.   I caught none
of half that size, but found it a thrilling experience to haul out a three pounder.   The best
bait is a live frog, and if they take it at all,
they dart upon it like a hawk.   Some days
they would not touch the bait, though I could
see plenty of them among the rocks, just
beneath me, in six feet of water.

I was very anxious to kill some grouse.
Their meat was said to be excellent; and, when
up among the pines hunting gray squirrels, I
had heard them drumming.   Having learned
something of their habits from Mr. Cahoon, I
one day rode up to the summit of the pine-
covered ridge, between the Kaweah and Tule
rivers, and soon heard them in different parts
of the woods.   I advanced toward the one

that seemed nearest, and over the best ground. But the source of the sound was so indefinite, both as to distance and precise direction, that I found it impossible to locate it. Then I selected another, and another, with no better result. Finally, I got where the sound seemed to come from all directions at the same time. After a long search, I saw and shot the bird. It weighed three pounds, and when eating it, I thought it was worth fourteen miles on horse-back, and several hours' hunting. Subsequently, I killed several, but in most cases I utterly failed to see them, after I had certainly found the tree in which they were. Sometimes they kept on drumming, while I was walking around and under the tree. I never before heard a sound that I could not locate its source, when near. In that, I often found it impossible. The male bird produces the noise with a prominent vocal apparatus at the neck, and they sit perfectly motionless, generally in a lofty pine or fir. The meat has a peculiar flavor, derived from the pine leaves and cones upon which they feed. The old

ones are very tough, and an experienced
hunter gave a new-comer a recipe for making
them tender.   It was as follows: "Boil them
for soup, three successive days, and on the
fourth, you can eat the meat."

On the 8th of May, I had taken a ramble
along a summit of a ridge running westward
from our camp.   After finding nothing, but
some empty tracks and beds of deer, and some
amusement in pushing rocks from the verge
of a precipice and seeing them whirl, and
smoke, and burst as they rushed among the
cracking brush in the gorge, three or four
hundred feet below, I went down into the
canyon and returned homeward.   In some
places there were small flats, grown over with
weeds and grass a foot high.   At others, the
steep, rocky, and brushy hill-sides closed
almost together, leaving the only path over
boulders and rocks, where, in winter, was a
torrent, then, only a feeble brook.

On one of the flats, I noticed an unusual
track upon the grass.   It looked a little like
the track of an unshod horse or bullock.

But the weeds and grass were very much dragged down from step to step. It might be a bear. But none had yet been seen in the neighborhood. However, he had to cross the brook, twenty yards ahead. The sand would tell. And there they were, "Foot-prints on the sands," but not so full of encouragement, as those of which the poet wrote. Bear stories are very laughable around the camp-fire, or a thousand miles away; but to a green hunter, in a deep rocky canyon, two miles from camp, and alone; a fresh bear-track is invested with impressive interest. There is poetry in that of a deer; none, in that of bruin. The print of every toe-nail looks like business. This at most, was only a few hours old. Appearances indicated only a few minutes. However, as it was going my only road, I concluded to slowly follow. With an ounce ball and nine buck-shot ready for instant use, "Betsy" advanced cautiously, and gave him time to get well on, if he was at all disposed so to do. Though, by the track, he was not over three hundred pounds weight, I was not anxious for a fight.

In the first place, there were no spectators, but the vultures soaring above. And spectators are a most important circumstance in a battle. For if you win, there is nobody to crown you; and if your opponent wins, being a bear, he would simply make "nuts and raisins" of your carcass; and all your friends would ever know about it would be that " He went out with the gun, and didn't come back."

Then, in the second place, I had on a new check shirt, which I could not well spare; and the print of those nails looked as if they would be hard on clothes. After passing a half mile of grass, brush, and boulders, the track turned into the Black Hill. I was satisfied.

But camp-life became monotonous. Mr. Cahoon's lessons took but an hour or two each day. I had been out in eight different directions, and knew all the trails and country for several miles around.

Along the Kaweah, for twenty miles, are strewn immense quantities of boulders, red-

wood, and pine logs. Some places they cover
the river-bed and adjoining flats, a half mile
wide, and are often piled up as high as fifteen feet.
Down on the plains, for many miles around,
the farmers split up the lumber for fencing
and building. They tried to saw it, but it
was too full of gravel. The boulders are
mostly granite, varying in size from a bird's
egg up to forty feet in diameter. The pines
and red-woods, too, were of all sizes, from
that of a bean up to logs ten feet in diameter,
and to ten, fifteen and even twenty feet in
length. Huge logs, eight feet in diameter, were
broken off like a pipe-stem, and of many, the
ends were rounded and pounded into a stumpy
splint broom. It was often a matter of wonder to me whence they all came, and I wanted
to see the quarry.

Mr. Cahoon was busy dressing deer skins.
Unable to get company, I determined to go
alone. Intending a trip northward, in June, I
had recently purchased a horse; so if accident
happened to horse or rider, the loss would be
all my own. He did not plainly advise me

8

not to go, but I saw that he thought it very doubtful whether the "parson" would make the whole trip. The trail led across the Sierra Nevadas to Owen's river, and had been travelled a good deal a few years before, but was then little used, and no one had yet been over it since winter; for on the summit, there were several feet of snow. Then there were five fords to cross, three of which were bad, and one really dangerous.

But looking up at those lofty mountains, from day to day, begets in one a desire to climb. As they frown down upon you, causing a painful sense of your mighty littleness, you draw a full breath, straighten, like the immortal Oliver, "pluck up a spirit," and say, "I will some day place my feet upon your highest peaks." Taking grub for two or three days, two heavy blankets, shawl and overcoat, and telling Mr. Cahoon if I did not return in four days, he might conclude I was fast, at 6.40, on Thursday morning, May 29th, I started. The ground I wished to reach was near the head waters of the Kaweah, and only fifteen miles from camp.   The first four I had been over, and the first six the trail was good.

This brought me to the second ford.   Here the mountains close abruptly in, and confine the trail to the river-bed.   Among the huge boulders it is mostly invisible, and is often found by its being the only practicable way ahead.   Getting through, and ascending the south bank, I found a fresh bear-track going in the same direction.   So there was company of some kind up there, at any rate.

By noon, I reached the third ford, the dangerous one.   I unsaddled and picketed my horse to eat a little grass growing among the brush and rocks.

Fifty feet beneath, through a narrow and frightful gorge the diminutive river tore its noisy way.   It was clear as glass, excepting where beaten to foam.

While thankfully eating a hearty lunch of graham bread and dried venison, I looked prayerfully down into the gorge, carefully down into my own heart, and hopefully up to the blue sky.

Having finished lunch, I went down and examined the ford. There were two; one terribly bad, the other still worse. The water was much higher than when Mr. Cahoon had crossed, according to the marks he gave me. The danger arose, not from the great amount of water, or the sharpness of the rocks, but from the swiftness of the former, and the unevenness and slipperiness of the latter. Mr. Cahoon had avoided riding over, by tying a stone to the end of his picket-rope, throwing it over, and then going around, jumping from rock to rock, getting over, and then leading his horse. But the height of the water now, rendered this impossible, and if I crossed, it must be on horseback. On a patch of sand, among the rocks, I saw the track of my friend bruin. Like myself, he seemed to have been examining the ford.

Saddling up, I led my horse down the narrow trail. Twenty feet from the river is an off-set, of about three feet, over a smooth rock. Bill refused to go down. I pulled forward, he backward. I went up and coaxed. He would

go to the brink, and then refuse. I set down
my gun, patted, and coaxed more. He would
not stir. I paused and considered. Probably,
the beast was right, as a dumber beast, bearing
a wiser prophet, was, on a certain occasion long
ago. Would it not be better to suffer defeat,
go back to camp, and report the ford impassable? I afterward learned, that an Indian
and an old mountaineer did that, a few days
later. But there was one means yet untried.
There were plenty of brush growing around,
and the rod sometimes exerts a healthy influence upon naughty creatures. So Solomon
thought, in reference to the genus homo. I
knew that he was not acquainted with Spanish
horses, or he might well have enlarged the
scope of his advice. I did what he had
neglected, and made the application. Bill
went down; I mounted, committed all to the
hands of the good Father, spurred down
another shelf into the current, with my feet
loosely in the stirrups, and ready to throw
"Betsy" away in a moment, if Bill should
stumble.

Six feet to the left, is a fall, of a few feet, over which horses and men have been swept. So uneven and glassy is the rock beneath, that if a horse falls, there is no hope for him. It is scarcely eight yards across, and in a half minute I was over, with my heart full of gratitude, and my shoes full of water. Pouring out the contents of both, I wrung out my socks and was soon climbing up the side of the gorge, leading my horse. He slipped, got a terrible fall, lay on his side and groaned, but broke no bones. The great danger was passed.

In a half-hour, the trail seemed to turn into the river again. In fact, it had "run out." The winter snows had bent down the brush above, and the grass had grown up from below. I lost an hour, got up into a brushy hill, and went until my horse could go no further. Leaving horse and gun, I crept through the brush, hunted for the trail, finally found it; by the vigorous use of a stout knife made a way for Bill, and was soon ready for something new. The trail zig zagged up a bare hill as steep as a gothic roof, rising nearly a thousand feet to get over a rocky bluff, then descending to the river again. Once more losing the trail, and an hour in finding it, and crossing two more fords, I then ascended the main ridge, the first of the mountains proper, and was soon among the pines.

The sun was getting low, and spiteful little snow-flakes came whirling down from a black cloud. My overcoat was comfortable. Up, up, up. The trail was now plain, and the timber fine. The only sounds were the roar of the river below, and the indefinite "woom! woom! woom!" of the motionless grouse, among the lofty pines above. Leaving the ascending trail, I kept on a level around the mountain side, to strike Mr. Cahoon's old camping place near the river. The view down the canyon and into the distant valley was magnificent. On the mountain side, alternate gulches and ridges ran down toward the main canyon. The surface was densely covered with wild tansy—a stubborn little shrub about knee high. Occasionally, there were little patches of grass. Four deer started up, ran across a gulch and a ridge, then stood. I got down and fired a ball, at about one hundred and fifty yards. One switched his tail, skipped around a turn or two, and then all trotted away. As they went toward my camping place, I rode on, and presently saw them standing looking at me. Again, I tried to get within range, but they kept well off. The wild tansy seemed to be no obstacle to them. It was a serious one to me, and I gave them up. As they emerged from another ravine, and passed with the ease of cloud-shadows over another ridge, I counted nine. They looked as though made for that grand mountain country, and it seemed almost wicked to disturb them.

At 7 o'clock, I reached the first "big tree," *sequoia gigantea*. Its sides were burnt out, and I saw at once that it would make a good camp. I unsaddled, picketed Bill, soon had a fire, a cup of tea, and a hearty supper. The thermometer marked 37°. The black clouds, like a flock of vultures, all sailed away, and as twilight faded beautifully out, the good old

robin, the blessed, plain old robin sang, from
the top of a lofty fir, its evening song. Whatever else may or may not be around, I am
sure God is always present where there are
robins.

My tree, as I found by tape-line, next morning, was fifty-two feet in circumference, and it
seemed as though it had been burned out for
a one man camp.   There was a good place for
my bed, and at the foot a small place for fire,
before which I put a shell of rock, and had an
elegant place to "toast my toes."   The grand
old pines, red-woods and firs stood around,
the river murmured just below, and the stars
shone brilliantly above.   But sweeter than all,
was the sublime silence. . At peep of day, the
robin sang his morning song.   Remembering
that "the early bird caught the worm," and,
what was of more importance to me, that deer
are early risers, at 4½ o'clock, I had fire made
and water on for tea.

I had just washed, and was wiping the sleep
well out of my eyes, when, looking out among
the pines, I saw a deer coming up from the

river, only a hundred yards away. Uncombed and hatless, I took "Betsy," and went out toward him. No wonder he fled! But "where there's one, there's more," came into my mind, and I went on. Up came another, and stood looking at me. Unable to hold the gun anywhere near steady, I fired a ball, at about seventy-five yards. He switched, walked up the hill a little way, and stood looking, as if trying to make out what kind of beast I might be.

I thought, "if you are so tame, I will go close and try buck-shot."

Getting a tree in range, I advanced. It trotted away. "Betsy" roared. It fell. I had roast tender-loin for breakfast. After breakfast, I skinned and hung up the meat to cool, which it soon did, with the mercury down at 27°.

Three of my nine shot had struck the game, one piercing the heart.

As I took my horse down to the river bank for better feed, about fifty yards below my camp, I found a new phenomenon—the unmistakable track of a grizzly bear. While *Ursus Major* had been making tracks in heaven above, *ursus horribilis* had been making them on earth below. Up to this time, I had been anxious to see a "grizzly" in the woods. Afterward, never; unless there were near me a tree easily climbed, or between us an unfordable stream. The track was ten by twelve inches, and was not extraordinary, for the bears have been killed weighing as much as eighteen hundred pounds. The track alone was sufficient for me.

I then went a half mile further up, to see the quarries, whence came the logs and boulders. I saw them. Vast mountain masses, a quarter of a mile in width, and some of them a half mile long; loosened by the rains and freighted with snow, had slipped out, bearing rocks, and trees, and all into the canyon. Then the river had dammed up, until the pressure overcame the resistance; then the whole ruin had been carried thundering and tearing down the mountain. Such evidences of hydraulic power, I had never before seen.

This branch of the river, here takes leaps of forty or fifty feet at a single bound. The snapping of logs, ten feet in diameter, and the rolling and polishing of boulders as large as a house, were fully explained.

Among the pines, I found a wonderfully beautiful flower. It was new to me, then, but I afterward learned that it is called the " snow flower," from the fact that it is found only at a high altitude, and appears soon after the snow melts. The botanist, John Torrey, says, it is a parasite, and names it, "*Sarcodes Sanguinea.*" It is deep crimson, shading off in its central parts into pink. It pushes through the soft granite soil, at once a marvel of beauty. A fleshy central peduncle, from three to ten inches in height, has thickly set all over it vasiform flowers about three-fourths of an inch in length, and among these, winding spirally upward, narrow, fleshy leaves of the same crimson color. The whole forms an outline not unlike an ear of indian corn. Not a green leaf appears. The whole expands a little, after

having attained its full height, and in a few
days, turns black and dies.

On another occasion, I found seven growing in a cluster, and digging down a foot,
I found a curious root composed of a mass
of little, soft, translucent bulbs. Like the
scarlet flamingo amid the dense green of
tropical forests, so these are in such striking
contrast with everything around, that they
would arrest the attention of the most careless.
I carried one home, but succeeded in preserv-
ing it only a few days.

After dinner, I boned the hams of my deer,
packed up twenty-one pounds of meat, as
much as I dared pack upon the horse, besides
myself, and then started homeward. Night
found me below the dangerous ford, camped
on the dry sand, in the river bed, among the
logs and boulders. A huge red-wood log
sheltered me from the wind blowing down the
canyon, and a lively fire roared at my feet.
As it threatened to reach an immense pile of
logs near by, at ten o'clock, I got up and rolled
some small ones out of the way. There was

danger of its getting to the adjoining hills, where much of the grass was already dry, and fires were likely to do damage. At four o'clock, I was awakened by a succession of reports, like dull pistol shots. Opening my eyes, I saw the hills lighted up, a volume of pitchy smoke ascending, and that huge pile of logs on fire. I had no time to lose in getting out. The red-woods were snapping like a battery of small Gatling guns, and the heated boulders were throwing hot hemispherical shells. To say that I "took up my bed and walked," would not describe the action. Bill was all right; picketed up on the hill-side, he ceased eating to see the moving. By rolling logs, and moving small wood, I cut off, as well as I could, the access of the fire to the mountain, ate a hearty breakfast, saddled up, and at 10½ o'clock, was back in camp. Mr. Cahoon was glad to see both me and meat, and gave me an invitation to live and hunt with him the coming winter. I was now initiated into the mysteries and luxuries of mountain life.

Nine days afterward, the folks in Grouse

Hunting among the Sierras.

Page 127.

Valley were out of meat. Doc had hunted
the surrounding hills in vain; so he proposed
an expedition up to the same country, where I
had seen so much game. I consented to go
along, if Mr. Cahoon would furnish two horses,
and run the risks. Bill was not only tired,
but badly bruised, also. He agreed, as we
were again nearly out of meat, too.

Now, as this hunt contains a precious, little
bear story, I must give details. We prepared
four or five days' "grub," and met by agreement down at the river, on Monday morning,
the ninth of June. There were Doc, Oliver,
his little brother, a lad of eleven years, who
went along to keep camp, and help look after
the horses, Billy Davis, a young man of
eighteen, and myself. Doc and his brother had
three horses, Billy and I, each two, one to ride,
and one with pack. We made a lively little
caravan, and as I had just been over the route,
we lost no time in hunting the trail. There
was some trembling at the dangerous ford,
and the more, because Doc had once seen a
man and horse carried over the rapids. But

we all got safely over. Three of the seven horses fell on the slippery rock, going up from the river.

Doc was very tall, and rode a high white horse, named "Gimlet." He often got fast in the incumbent brush. Then we all halted until "Gimlet" bored through. For Doc, the boring was more than merely disagreeable. When we got through those brushy hills, his face and ears were bleeding. For the smallest of us, on the lower horses, it was rough. The process is this : You come up to a tight place, and your horse halts. You draw your slouch hat down, lean forward along-side the horn of the saddle, with your face by the horse's mane, hold your gun in the right hand, with muzzle to the ground, when in company, with the left hold the rein, or the horn of the saddle, spur the beast, and tell him to go along. He thrusts forward his muzzle, lays back his ears, and obeys orders. Then you feel about like an ear of corn going through a corn-sheller. On my previous trip, I was nearly raked from the saddle several times, and once my gun was discharged. A good slouch hat, heavy duck coat, and overalls, are the only security against a large collection of very un-profitable rents.

At four, P. M., we reached camp. The others had a small tent. I camped in the hollow of a fallen "big tree" near by, prefer-ing the open air. Next day, all, excepting Oliver, went out to hunt. Billy, south, on foot; Doc, east, on "Gimlet;" I, on "Barney," went up the Owens River trail, and struck for the summit. Just then, I was more interested in the scenery than in game. About 9½ o'clock, I rode out upon the rocky crest of the first mountain, in the main chain of the Sierra Nevadas. The altitude was about eight thou-sand feet. The red-woods had disappeared. A few pines and firs stood feebly around. Be-yond, on the flat, the timber was mostly "tamarack." Beneath, and westward, was the grandest extensive view I ever saw. Just be-low, were the high hills and deep canyons, covered with lofty pines, firs and red-woods. Below these, and receding toward the plains,

9

thirty miles away, were the foot-hills, already burned brown by the sun. Below all, was the valley of the San Joaquin, partly hidden by clouds. A little to the south of west, seventy miles distant, like a silver cloudlet, lay Tulare Lake. Toward it wound the green water-courses of the Tule, Kaweah, and Kings rivers. In the haze, bounding the western horizon, stretched the Coast Range. To the east, rose majestic snow-covered peaks, five thousand feet higher than where I stood. The sky was cloudless above, and the air exhilarating. I uncovered my head and thanked God for, the providence that had led me to that spot. "Deep answereth to deep." The depth of trial, to the summit of earthly blessing. It seemed but a little way to heaven—much nearer than Babel builders ever get.

Turning eastward, through the standing and many prostrate tamaracks, I was soon among the snow-drifts—the remains of the mighty piles that had been stored there during the previous winter. I travelled on, about four miles, over minor ridges, and then entered

some broad meadows. The snow had just
disappeared from these, and the grass was
peeping through. I left the trail, turned northward, made a circuit, struck a chain of little
lakes, found, and shot a lone mallard duck, but
saw no other game, and only a few tracks of
deer. The day was beautiful; the thermometer rose to 70° at noon. I picketed my horse
upon a grassy plot, and sat down by a snow-
cold brook to enjoy my lunch. The least
expected annoyance in the world now developed itself, and became serious. The
mosquitoes were thick enough to have made
a Jerseyman feel perfectly at home. Several
contended at once for a choice spot upon my
nose. Often, while in the east, have I men-
tally sung the "doxology," after finding and
slaying, in the dark hours of night, one of
these dreadful pests, at which I had long and
vainly slapped. Here, to kill them was easy.
They never moved when once they settled.
It was a favorable place to take cheap ven-
geance upon the whole race. Returning to
camp, I met the others going out for a deer,

that Doc had killed in the morning. Billy had seen no game. My duck was the first meat brought in, but it was only "duck-meat."

Next day, we hunted again. Doc saw nothing. Billy saw a bear, a great way off across a canyon. I travelled about eight miles on foot, purposely for game, and got one grouse, and three severe tumbles among the rocks and brush. I went through some fearful country, saw plenty of deer tracks and some signs of bear.

As the bears had devoured the carcass of the deer I had killed, when there before, I determined to set my gun for them over night. I got into camp about sundown, took the trimmed carcass of Doc's deer, and went a quarter of a mile down the canyon, so as to be certainly out of the way of two horses which were not picketed. Going over the edge of a deep ravine, which opened into a still larger one, densely covered with brush, rocks, and live oaks, I found a small fallen tree-top and a clump of bushes and rocks near by, which furnished a suitable place to fix the bait.

The wind had already set down the canyon, and I kept a good look-out down in that direction, not knowing but that I might get a customer before I was ready. Having fixed the bait so it could be reached in only one direction, I tied "Betsy" in the tree-top, with three stout cords and straps. To the triggers I adjusted small levers, and to them a heavy trout-line, so as to fire both barrels at once. I had fastened my line, drawn it to the proper tension, and was ready to cock the gun and leave. At that moment, I heard a cracking in the bushes just above, where I had come down, and looked up, thinking one of the horses had found me. Horrors! There was coming down, right for me, a brown bear! His nose was toward the ground, and he was coming over the wild tansy in an easy gallop. He evidently wanted *my carcass.*

Without the least intention of being polite on my part, my hat rose, I should think, near-ly an inch. "Betsy" was securely tied. I had no pistol, nor even a sheath-knife. My vocal organs were very defective. However, they uttered a respectable "booh-wooh!" The credit for the first part of that very natural expression belongs wholly to the bear, and I will not attempt to deprive him of it. But the second, I am conscious of having willed. He dropped upon his haunches, looked at me, seemed to be frightened about as badly as myself, or else, sorry that he had so badly scared me, turned and ran down the hill. In a few seconds I had "Betsy" cut loose, and followed him over the edge of the ravine, only to hear the brush crack down below. It was now too late to readjust my gun, and thinking he might come back, or another come along attracted by the smell of the meat, I mounted some rocks near by, got well out of danger, and watched my bait as long as I could see to shoot. Then I trudged slowly back to camp, tired and without game, but happy in forever having a patent right to a bear story of my own, without *inventing it*. I shall always accord to that bear, great credit for his unexceptionable conduct.

Next morning, we concluded to go over the

dividing ridge, reach the head waters of the Tule river, and go home another way. We would thus avoid the dangerous ford, and more likely get game.

Doc was thoroughly discouraged. He had calculated upon killing, at least, a half dozen deer himself.

Billy and Oliver had finished breakfast and had strolled away.

Doc and I were washing down the last bites of bread with the nether contents of the coffee-pot. Billy came hastily and quietly back, saying: "There's a bear coming down the hill." Doffing coats and donning arms, we went out to meet him. Sure enough, there he was, slowly coming down among the pines and wild tansy, only eighty yards away, and heading for a point about forty yards distant. As he looked so stupid, and we had the wind, I advised to let him come closer. Billy and Doc dropped upon one knee, side by side, and when he was about seventy yards away, both rifles cracked together. He plunged forward, and was hidden behind a bank. As they began to re-load, I ran across the ravine before us, and when I rose upon the opposite bank, there he was, running straight on down on three legs. Letting him come full broad-side, I fired a ball at twenty paces. He tumbled over, gave a loud groan, and when I came up, he was in "articulo mortis." A ball from one of the rifles had pierced the superior muscles of his neck, and broken his right shoulder. Mine had gone square through his vitals and lodged against the skin. So it nearly happened, that "me and 'Betsy' killed a bear."

He was a cinnamon or brown bear, and though he looked large when running, he weighed only about two hundred pounds. We skinned him, hung up the meat to cool, and then concluded to return the way we came. Night found us at home again.

Having determined upon a journey, north-ward, on horseback, I made a pair of buck-skin saddle-bags, packed up my traps, and on Saturday, June 21st, bade good-bye to Mr. Cahoon and my mountain home. He had done well in orthography, and was able to write me a letter in a good plain hand, which he has since frequently done. I presented him a pocket Bible for a keep-sake, and he gave me his good old canteen. If he, during life's journey, draws as precious draughts of living water from that Book, as I drew from that canteen, during more than five hundred miles of a horseback ride over the hot plains and among the mountains, we shall have reason to be eternally grateful to each other.

CHAPTER V.

THE BIG TREES.

LIKE the hair upon some heads, the timber in California is concentrated upon particular spots. And as if to make up for the vast areas that are entirely bare, in those particular spots, there is a remarkable development. While the State, with all its variety, both of latitude and climate, does not grow hard timber fit for a wagon wheel or an axe handle, yet some of the soft woods attain to a size and clearness of grain, found in no other part of our country.

Before walking around, and measuring the "Big Trees" proper, we will spend a little time among the "red-woods." These are found on the mountains in all parts of the State, but in greatest perfection in the northern coast counties.

138

While in Mendocino county, I had an opportunity of passing through the entire belt to the sea coast, at the mouth of Big river. While to the eye, from the mountain summits about Little Lake, the whole country toward the coast appears generally level, yet, when one travels across, it proves to be covered with hills and cut by deep canyons.

The depth of the latter is often very deceptive, owing to the extraordinary height of the red-woods growing in their bottoms. Here, they have the steep hill-sides to protect, an alluvial soil of great depth and living springs to nourish from below, and the daily fogs from the ocean to supply them moisture from above. They range through all diameters up to ten and even twelve feet. Diameters of six and seven feet are very frequent. Heights of two hundred and fifty and two hundred and seventy feet are common. Some have been felled, measuring three hundred and twenty-five. They are nearly always straight as an arrow, mostly perpendicular, and often more than one hundred feet clear of limbs. It is no unusual thing for a single tree to cut thirty thousand feet of lumber.

On the coast, at the mouth of the stream, whence the lumber is shipped in schooners, they erect a saw-mill, work inland felling trees, saw them into convenient lengths, roll them into the stream, float them down, and, with a boom, prevent them running out to sea. When they get above reach of the tides, or during the season of low water, they fill the channel with logs, and wait for the winter's freshet. When the main canyon is cleared of choice timber, they work into the lateral ravines, lay skids, keep them wet, bark the logs, attach oxen, and drag them down to the river-bank.

At Big River, this work has been going on nineteen years. The quantities cut and shipped are almost incredible. When I was there, owing to decreased demand, they were running only half their saws, and yet they cut twenty-six thousand feet per day. They had worked up the river, following its devious course more than forty miles, and up at the head-waters, when hunting, I found their lines of skids extending up side ravines, a full mile from the river-bank. These skids are sometimes laid lengthwise with the ravine, nearly even with the surface of the ground, and about two feet apart, but generally they are laid crosswise, and about six feet apart.

Owing to the scarcity of water, the winter previous, the whole year's cutting was yet lying in the river-bed. Some places you could walk two miles, stepping from log to log. There was a man placed in charge, who rode from point to point, to protect them from fire, that might accidentally break out from the camps of hunters, teamsters, or travellers. He told me, there were then about twelve millions of feet ready to be floated down. To insure its going, they had built a twenty-foot dam across a canyon, which they could open at the opportune moment, and sweep the whole mass through, in a few hours.

The felling of one of these trees is worth a journey to witness. The best ground in the circle is selected, and often it has to be leveled up to prevent breaking the tree. Very often neighboring trees or stumps are so numerous that it is necessary to strike a particular line. If the trunk, a hundred feet from the stump, falls a single foot from that line, it may spoil a hundred dollars worth of lumber.

The ground is chosen, and the tree plumbed. If it varies at all from the perpendicular, proportionate allowance must be made in the direction of the first notch. A scaffold is erected six, eight, or ten feet high, depending upon the character of the "butt."

Many of the trees taper rapidly from the ground, up to six or ten feet, and even then the first log is, occasionally, so dense that it has to season several years before it will float in water.

The chopper mounts the scaffold and begins work. If it is Monday morning, the tree eight feet in diameter, and he does good work, on Tuesday afternoon, you will feel the ground shake and hear hoarse thunder.

I had often heard them, when six miles away, and once waited a good while to see one fall. The first notch is cut in, a little beyond the centre, and a wooden instrument used to determine the precise direction. It is made of two narrow boards about six feet long. At the middle of one, the end of the other is fixed at right angles. The first being placed carefully and tightly up in the notch, the medial line in the other, at the centre of the tree, must point precisely to the spot, one hundred or one hundred and fifty feet away, where the centre of the trunk is to strike.

When the tree is not quite perpendicular, or when the few limbs are not equally distributed, it is an exceedingly nice point to calculate.

In the fall I witnessed, the tree was six and a half feet in diameter, two hundred and seventy feet high; and it fell within a few inches of the line intended.

To see the fall of an unfinished structure, that had commenced building two hundred years before Columbus discovered America, was really exciting. Standing off at a safe distance, as the feeble blows of the chopper were severing the last two or three inches of support, a company of us intently watched the top, to see the very first movement. It was perfectly calm there in the silent canyon. There was not only no swaying, but not even the least vibration. Like a king, it stood perfectly poised in grand and regal majesty.

It's going at last! No! The eye is deceived. It was the light cloud far above. The suspense is almost painful. Now it moves! Does it not? Yes, but so slowly that you almost fear to say yes. Now faster! The chopper clambers down. What a mighty sweep! It leaps forward ten feet from the stump, and strikes the earth with its whole length and weight.

The force of the fall is so great, that they sometimes split, and when the sap is running, and they are felled down a slope, they sometimes shoot clean out of their bark.

And now, as to the "Big Trees," properly so called—for naturalists say they are a different species. About the only difference, visible to an ordinary observer, is in the leaf. That of the red-wood is flat, like the leaf of "arbor vitae," while that of the "*Sequoia Gigantea*" is like that of the cedar.

Having heard that the largest tree in the State was in the Tulare Grove, Tulare Co., forty-five miles north-east of Visalia, I determined to see it, if possible.

As it would not add more than sixty miles to my horseback ride, north, through the State, I made arrangements with Rev. Mr. Parker, of the Baptist Church, in Visalia, to visit the monster in company.

We set out, at noon, on Monday, June 23d. The first night we spent with a friend near the foot-hills. The second, we camped in a deserted cabin, up among the pines. The next morning, we rose early, had pressing need of our overcoats, ate a frugal breakfast, and started for "Mill Flat." Supposed to be an experienced mountaineer, by that time, I accepted the responsibility of finding the road, but lost it, and was set right by the workmen in a shingle camp.

We found the Flat, picketed our horses, and undertook the remaining mile on foot.

10

Sheep, just from the plains, ninety miles distant, had obliterated the trail. However, we lost but little time in finding the first "big tree." It proved to be "The Old Maid." She stands lonely and alone. A few years ago, some ungallant speculators, not having the fear of Uncle Sam before their eyes, intended to remove a section of her, for exhibition. Workmen began to girdle her, not with gold, but steel; the land agent at Visalia, heard of it, served an injunction upon them, and prevented a case of monstrous kidnapping. The girdle is about her yet, but her health does not seem to be affected, and she is green and flourishing in her old age. I encircled her with my tape-line, a few feet above ground. She measured 85 feet, 10 inches.

We set out to hunt the other trees, got separated; and when I had lost Mr. Parker, I found the West Grove. Here the largest, from its venerable appearance, had been named "Adam." The cruel fire had cleft him down at one side, presenting a charred wall twenty feet wide, and in the centre, about twelve feet high. However, at four feet above ground, he girthed 71 feet.

I then gave up the trees, and hunted for Mr. Parker, followed the trail up the mountain, a full mile, and met a hunter, who put me on the route to find the East Grove.

Supposing now, that Mr. Parker was really lost, I ate my lunch alone, and then found the remaining trees. There are more than fifty, but, by far the largest, is the "General Grant." One of the next largest, is the "General Lee," of which a section has been promised for the Centennial Exhibition. The "Gen. Grant" is probably the largest single-trunked tree in the world. It is straight, clear of limbs nearly one hundred feet, has a well-proportioned top, and is well preserved. At the base, however, it spreads out into great "humps." Upon some of these, you can climb up, eight or ten feet. Fire, too, has marred the symmetry of the ground plan. A carpenter, at Visalia, estimated that it contained eight hundred thousand feet of lumber. Its height is about two hundred and fifty feet. I applied my tape-line about four feet above ground, and found the circumference to be one hundred and four feet, three inches, giving a diameter of over thirty-three feet.

Having paid my respects to the President, I walked into, and through a fallen giant, named "Napoleon." The heart, and underside, had been burned out. The papers said, that five men could ride in abreast, pass through the trunk sixty feet, and then ride out at a "knot-hole." A man told me that he had "ridden through, and, when inside, could just reach the top of the arch with his riding whip." After taking some dimensions, I at first concluded, that other products than trees, grew to an abnormal size, in that country. But I had in mind, the average Pennsylvania horse, and a riding whip in proportion. Second thought reduced the length of the whip, as well as the height and thickness of the probable California horse. Some of those Spanish mustangs, are not much thicker than a Delaware shad, and the feet of a tall man, when in the stirrups, nearly touch the ground.

So the statement may be literally true. And the knot-hole story, cannot be disproved; for, after riding along about sixty feet, a careful "dodger" might safely pass out, where the side of the tree has been burned away. Of course, the "knot-hole," might have been *burned up!*

Returning toward the Flat, I again met the hunter, who told me that Mr. Parker had given up the search, and turned homeward.

I followed and overtook him, at our old camping place. He had found the West Grove, had spent some time in company with "Adam," gave me up as lost, concluded that "General Grant" was not to be seen that afternoon, and returned to the horses. The hunter came along, and told him that his companion was safe, and likely to see the President. I teased him a little about riding ninety miles, to visit such a distinguished individual, and then failing to get an introduction.

We spent the night with Peter Pepin, a Frenchman, distantly related to King Charlemagne. And royally were we entertained.

Excellent feed for our horses, good "grub" for ourselves, and the downy luxury of a hay-mow for a bed.

The next day, we travelled together, six miles further down the mountain, when Mr. Parker returned toward Visalia, and I continued my journey northward, alone. Twenty-three miles more of mountain and foot-hill, brought me down to the plains at Fowler's Ranch, on King's River, opposite to Centreville. It was Thursday night. I now had one hundred and thirty-four miles to the Mariposa Big Trees. The next two days' ride was mostly over the bare, burning plains. The grass and flowers had grown and ripened. What had not been eaten by the thousands of cattle, and ten thousands of sheep, had been swept away by the wind. Nothing remained but the seeds that had fallen into the deep cracks made by the hot sun. The stock had gathered about the water-courses, or had been driven to the mountains. An occasional shade tree was a luxury. I always lay by, a few hours, at noon. The thermometer frequently ran above 100°;

once to 115°, in the shade. I was glad to get among the foot-hills and mountains again.

On the following Tuesday, I reached Clark & Moore's Ranch, at the terminus of the stage-road from Mariposa to Yosemite.

It is six miles by trail out to the Mariposa Big Trees. I concluded to spend the night among them. Clark & Moore's is four thousand one hundred and forty-one feet above the sea. The grove is two thousand two hundred feet higher. The lonely ride was grand, the trees magnificent.

There are really two groves, a lower and an upper. I cared chiefly to see the largest tree. One of the finest, bears the name of "La Fayette." It is eighty-three feet in circumference, and beautiful in proportion. A prostrate tree is called the "Fallen Giant." It is eighty-five feet in circumference, and is supposed to be fifteen hundred years old.

The largest in the grove is the "Grizzly Giant." It is a ponderous tree, but the top is very imperfect, and the height is not equal, by more than fifty feet, to that of the "General

Grant." Between fifteen and eighty feet, I should think, the diameters of the two are very nearly alike.

About eighty feet from the ground, a huge limb projects about twenty-five feet, and then turns up at right angles. It has been compared to a boxer "showing the muscle" of his arm. A civil engineer measured it, and found the diameter of the limb near the trunk to be six feet. The guide books say, "The circumference of the tree, seven-and-a-half feet above ground, is seventy-eight-and-a-half feet, and three feet above ground, over one hundred. About four feet above ground my tape-line said, ninety feet.

To indicate fairly the size, most of these "Big Trees" ought to be measured from ten to fifteen feet above ground. A few have no "humps" at the base, but most of them have such an enormous lateral development near the ground, that to measure them there gives a very false impression of the size of the tree.

While my good old mountain friend, the robin, sang his evening song, I picketed

Bill, gave him the barley I had brought from
Clark & Moore's, prepared and ate my own
evening meal, spread my blankets upon a bed
of fir branches near the foot of the "Grizzly
Giant," and sweetly lay down to rest. Over
me was stretched that mighty bared arm, re-
minding me of an infinitely mightier, around
and underneath me.

It is written, that "it is not good for man to
be alone." But it does not say, that it is not
good for *a* man to be alone. If it did I should
doubt the authority. Who that has tried it will
say that it is not good, occasionally in a noisy
lifetime, to get away from the habitations of
busy men, above the region of fogs, among the
modest birds, and timid wild beasts, and stately
trees, and shadowy mountains! Upon this natural gothic magnificence, there are everywhere
inscribed the words:—"The Lord is in his holy
temple, let all the earth keep silence before
him." The night was wonderfully short.
During one solid "nap" the world had turned
around, and daylight came creeping down
those "long drawn aisles."

Six-and-a-half o'clock found me back at Clark & Moore's. A good breakfast, a pleasant company of tourists, and some familiar names on the register, were all refreshing.

It was only twenty-three miles to Yosemite. That day's light was to reveal to me the wonder of wonders. Indeed, the "Seven Wonders" are now condensed into one. So the guide books seemed to teach.

But before leaving the subject of "Big Trees," I should state, the Calavaras Grove, north-west of Yosemite, is the best known. They were first discovered, and there is a good stage-road the whole distance. The tallest tree in the grove is the "Keystone State." It is three hundred and twenty-five feet high, but only forty-five feet in circumference. A few years ago, the largest one was cut down. After being bored entirely off, about six feet above ground, it refused to fall, and had to be wedged over. Five men worked at it twenty-one days. It is not recorded how hard they worked. The stump was smoothed off, and covered with a pavilion. It is twenty-seven feet in diameter, without the bark, and contains one thousand two hundred and twenty-five annular growths.

There is a grove, also, in Fresno county, one of which was felled several years ago. I conversed with a man who helped two others in felling it. After they had worked five days, in digging under and chopping off the roots, the monster toppled over. They riveted together three eight-foot cross-cut saws, and cut off a section, the outer portion of which, divided into pieces, they carried away for exhibition. It was twenty-three feet in diameter.

In Tulare county, a few miles south of the grove containing the "General Grant," there is said to be a stump forty-five feet in diameter. The top is entirely gone. Fierce fires occasionally sweep through the mountains, burn up the dead, and greatly mar the living trees. By many these are supposed to be the largest trees in the world. And while none have been discovered that excel them in every respect, yet there are some that exceed them, each in one particular. In Australia there is

a species that, with very moderate height, has
been found with a diameter of eighty-one feet.
Another, with comparatively small diameter,
reaches the enormous height of four hundred
and eighty feet.

CHAPTER VI.

THE trail from Clark's to Paragoy's is said to be eleven miles. It seemed to me more like *twenty*. As a specimen of crookedness, double-twisted, it is hard to surpass. At the end of the ride, one may truly say, "I have had my ups and downs." But, as is not always the case, the "ups" exceed the "downs" by about three thousand feet. The scenery, though not sublime, is grand. From the mountain sides, you get rare glimpses of wooded hills and deep canyons, of sparkling streams, dashing down through narrow gorges, and magnificent groves of sugar-pine and fir.

At Paragoy's, there are two trails to the valley. One, leading nearly directly north, enters the western or lower end by way of "Inspiration Point." The other, north-east, by

157

way of "Sentinel Dome" and "Glacier Point."
Advice from those who had been over both,
determined me to take the latter. To "Glacier
Point" was six miles. The trail led across a
number of flats from which the last snow had
disappeared only three days before, though it
was then the second day of July.

Several times, my horse came very near
miring. When I had gone four miles, "Sentinel Dome" hove in sight. It is a massive
hemisphere of solid granite, almost as regular
as the dome of a cathedral, and it rises several
hundred feet above the country surrounding
it on the south side.

From its base down to "Glacier Point" is
about a mile, over a rough trail, having a descent of about one thousand feet. I feared
the point would be too low to afford a good
view of the valley. Having already been disappointed in some of the California wonders,
I was expecting a repetition of it here. It was
six o'clock when I tied Bill to one of the few
trees, took out my spy-glass and walked out
upon the extremity of the rock. The sun

shone clearly, but the silence was almost oppressive. The tourist of the day had been
there and gone. Not even a bird warbled an
evening song.

The first attractive object was "Yosemite
Fall," about one-and-a-half miles north-west,
leaping lightly over the northern rim of the
valley. The verge from which it plunged is
about on a level with the "Point." To the
north-east, about the same distance, was
"Half Dome." On its bald summit of solid
granite lay a patch of snow. Around further
to the right, rose "Mount Broderick," or "The
Cap of Liberty." Near it was "Nevada Fall,"
and below that, "Vernal Fall." Sweeping
around again toward the west, to the left of
"Yosemite Fall," you recognize the "Three
Brothers," and further down still, on the north
side, the unmistakable form of "El Capitan."
Directly west, on the south side of the valley,
a mile away, and rising a few hundred feet
above the point where you stand, is "Sentinel
Rock."

The size of the valley is surprising. I had

thought of it being only two or three miles long. But there before your eyes are the land marks. From "Glacier Point," north, to the opposite rim, is about three-quarters of a mile. From "El Capitan" to "Half Dome" is not less than four miles. At "Half Dome," the valley forks. The northern, and smaller, contains "Mirror Lake," and is called "Little Yosemite." Down the southern, from those lofty snow-covered summits, away to the east of you, flows that crystal child of snow, the "Merced." In its descent, about three miles above "Half Dome," it forms the "Nevada" and "Vernal Falls." The whole length of the valley is seven miles.

But we have not yet seen the bottom! Have you a cool and steady head? You will need it here.

The rock is bare, and level enough, but there is no balustrade. Take it gradually. Look down at an angle of thirty-five degrees. Do you see that little lake in "Little Yosemite?" Can it be water? It looks like polished steel, partly shaded now, for it will reflect the

sun no more to-day. That is "Mirror Lake."
The Indians named it "Ke-ko-tu-yem"—
"Sleeping Water!" It has only seven acres of
surface, and is not over twenty feet deep. But
what a surface! and what a frame for a mirror!
How easily an old Greek would have throned
a god upon the summit of "Half Dome," just
four thousand seven hundred and forty feet
above, have seen him bathe his temples in the
fleecy cloud about his head, and bend over
that Mirror to see divinity reflected! Run
your eye on down the northern side of the
valley, beneath those "Royal Arches," suggestive of a masonry mighty and free—the
"Hun-to," or "Watchful Eye," of the Indian!
Come nearer to the awful verge. See the
"Merced," like a ribbon of silver, winding down
through the meadows. The houses seem to
be about the size of dog-kennels. You look
well down into their diminutive chimneys,
whence a dim smoke issues, rises a little way
toward you, and vanishes. There are some
dark specks, that look like heaps of hay in a
well defined field. There are winding roads

11

and bridges, and horsemen, wagons, and pack trains moving along upon them.   But roads and bridges, trees and houses, look like the playthings that a child arranges upon the floor, and the animals very similar to those which the same little fat hands bring out of the modern Noah's Ark.   Their odd appearance arises largely from the unusual direction in which you look at them.   The view is such as the aeronaut has from his balloon, and they are just two thousand six hundred feet beneath you.

The Indians call this point "Oo-uoo-yoo-wah"—"The great rock of the Elk."   If you drop a stone over the edge, just here, it will fall sixteen hundred feet, before striking the debris below.

With my glass I examined the objects more minutely, as the prominent ones at the upper end of the valley reflected the setting sun.

"Nevada Fall" presented a magnificent appearance.   The leap is *seven hundred* feet. You strain your ears to hear it, but vainly, for the breeze is yet setting up the valley.

Further down is the "Vernal Fall." It is four hundred and fifty feet. It was beautifully named by the Indians, "Pi-wy-ack"— "Shower of Crystals."

Turning again down the valley, I looked more carefully at the "Yosemite Fall." It is a marvel of beauty. Shooting clear over the bare, perpendicular, granite rim of the valley, like Niagara, at the American side, it turns at once to spray. Very unlike Niagara, however, it cannot be over fifty or sixty feet wide, when it first clears the verge. White as the foam on the pail of fresh milk, it forms into clouds, and these descend with the ease and apparent slowness of the volumes of smoke rising from a chimney on a calm morning. And often, with the eye, you can follow these separate clouds from top to bottom. Timing them twice, I found it took twenty seconds. The height of the first fall is *one thousand five hundred* and *eighty-seven* feet. Then tumbling over a rocky slope, six hundred and twenty-six feet further, it takes a final plunge of four hundred and twenty-eight feet.

Shadows were now covering the whole bottom of the valley. I had yet four miles of steep trail before supper and rest.

Turning westward toward "Sentinel Rock," I entered the new trail, dismounted, got a stick and drove Bill down before me. At the sharp elbows of the trail, he often stopped and examined for a side pass, but never with success.

Many suppose that a road constantly down hill is very easy to travel. Bill and I both concluded otherwise, at the end of the first mile.

In one weary hour, I again heard the sounds of the lower world, and came to a summer house gaily perched upon a prominent rock, with the stars and stripes floating proudly over it. At the end of the second hour, I reached the bottom. Those four miles are more road under less sky than any four consecutive miles I ever traveled. It was after nine o'clock when I reached Hutchings' Hotel.

A good night's rest, a beautiful morning, an excellent breakfast of speckled trout and

other good things, prepared me to look around
and up.

On the river bank nearly in front of the
hotel, were two Indians catching trout. I
witnessed the process with interest. The water
was four or five feet deep, swift, and clear as
crystal. The color of the gravel and boulders
upon the bottom gave it a slightly yellowish
hue. They baited with a small piece of a
large sucker. As the hawk darts upon its
prey, so those beautiful fish took the bait, and,
as gracefully as either, the young Indian flung
four of every five upon the bank. They ranged
from four to eight inches in length. Upon
the hotel porch, lay a string of them, weighing
ten pounds. They were just from the river
on their way to the pan.

Some tourists were rigging tackle to try
their luck. But it is said that the Indians
always excel. There is some kind of a
"league," not only between them and the
"beasts of the field," but also the fish of the
streams. As the mother pigeon feeds her
young with prepared food, so these Indians

will partially masticate even worms, to make a tempting bait for these wily denizens of the crystal flood.

This was the third of July. On the "Fourth," there was to be a celebration in the valley. At Clark & Moore's I had seen an enormous poster, announcing the fact and giving an outline of the edifying exercises.

The following items of interest were included:

1. An Indian was to ascend a rocky cliff at the "Yosemite Fall," and "plant the American flag where human foot had never trod."

2. There was to be a "sack race," by several men of eminent ability in that progressive art.

3. A chase after a "greased pig"—the captor to hold the prize!

When I spoke of seeing the valley that day and leaving, a gentleman expressed surprise that I did not "remain to see the celebration." I remarked that that was my chief reason for leaving, and that anybody who could descend to such business, in such a place, ought to leave the country.

Having previously studied a plan of the valley, and having had a general view from "Glacier Point," at eight o'clock, I mounted Bill, acted as my own guide, and rode up to "Mirror Lake," passing the "Royal Arches" to my left, and under the dark shadow of "Half Dome" to my right.

At the entrance to "Little Yosemite," and well up toward the lake, are immense masses of rock, which had evidently fallen from the impending cliffs on either side. The trail surmounted and wound among them. Had it not been, that they seemed to have fallen ages ago, and for the large trees and brush growing upon them, it would take a stout heart to pass up that gorge without hesitation.

At the lake, among the rocks and fir trees, was a small excursion house with boats and fishing tackle. A young gentleman and lady were out in a boat. The waves they made threw the granite walls beyond into moving folds.

Returning by way of Hutchings', I passed down the northern side of the valley, and had a near and new view of "Yosemite Fall." That volume of foam that was swayed by the morning breeze, and seemed so misty in the distance, makes grand music when you are near, and forms a swift stream, twenty-feet wide, that sweeps well up your saddle girth at the ford.

A little further down, I had a good view of "Sentinel Rock," on the south side of the valley, and caught occasional glimpses of the trail by which I had descended the previous evening. "Sentinel Rock" is a magnificent pile, three thousand and forty-three feet in height. Though it appears to stand well out from the top of the southern wall, yet its very summit may be reached from the rear.

Lower down, I met the "Three Brothers." They rise out of the northern wall, and each of the rear ones seems to be leaning forward, as though to look over the other's shoulder. They are three thousand eight hundred feet high, and from their peculiar position, the Indians named them, "Pom-pom-pa-sue"— "Mountains playing leap-frog."

To my left, now, were the "Cathedral Rocks" and "Cathedral Spires;" the former, two thousand six hundred and sixty, and the latter, two thousand four hundred feet in height.

But the king of all these kingly forms was now just ahead, to my right, viz: "El Capitan." The Indians call it, "Tu-tok-ah-nu-lah"— "The Great Chief of the Valley."

This cliff has two faces, one fronting a little to the east of south, the other a little west. The south-eastern face is a full half mile long, horizontally, joining in one seamless granite wall with the northern side of the valley. The western, is only half so long, and bends around more abruptly. The height is three thousand three hundred feet, and in places, it is not only perpendicular, but it leans slightly over the base. No description can do it justice. I have studied both photographs, paintings, and word pictures. Actual sight is necessary. Then, it is not only *seen*, but also, *felt*.

It is said, that a man familiar with the

scenery at Niagara, took a stranger friend from point to point, and failed to get from him any expression of surprise. The American Fall was viewed from Goat Island. It was "quite pretty." They looked at the Horseshoe Fall from Terrapin Tower. "Yes, it is considerable of a fall."

Hoping to get him overwhelmed with admiration in some way, as a last resort, he took him below. They looked up. Not a word of surprise. Indeed, he seemed to be surprised that anybody could get surprised at it.

"But don't you see that tremendous body of water pouring over those huge rocks?"

"Ye-yes. I don't see anything to *hinder it!*"

Whatever be the experience at Niagara, that in the presence of "El Capitan" will greatly differ, both in nature and degree. While the former may fitly represent the force, the dash, and the noisy roar of the human and changeable, the latter silently proclaims the reserved omnipotence and eternity of the Divine!

Think a few moments. Look at those
spruce and fir trees, growing on the debris at
the base. Cut off the limbs, and take that tall
one for a measuring stick. It is one hundred
and fifty feet high. Both to see clearly, and
for the comfort of your neck, stand back a
quarter of a mile. Apply the measuring rod.
Shove it up, length by length, as the carpenter
uses his rule to measure the height of a wall.
Now, carefully. One, two, three, four, five,
six, seven, eight, nine, ten! Rest a little. You
are now up one thousand five hundred feet—
as high as six tall church steeples, one on top
of the other. Now again: one, two, three,
four, five, six, seven, eight, nine, ten! You
are out of breath and chilly. We must hasten.
Three hundred feet more, and here we are
upon the summit. There is a cloud about
our heads. The brain grows dizzy. Descend.

Try another plan. You have been over
your neighbor's farm. It contains one hundred acres. It is quite a territory. Add to
it four more farms of the same size. Clear

off from these five hundred acres all the trees, fences, and buildings. Leave nothing but the bare ground, slightly rolling, and imagine that turned into solid granite, almost without a crevice. Now you have a surface about three-fourths of a mile each way. Dig it loose from the surrounding country all around. Under-mine it. Get a hundred thousand giants, with a hundred thousand jack-screws, and set it up plumb, on edge! You have the face of "El Capitan!"

While riding along that northern wall, and looking up at those revelations of infinite strength, I realized, as never before, the force of the Scripture: "Which by his strength setteth fast the mountains, being girded with power." Ps. lxv. 6. Previously, when among impending cliffs, I had breathed a prayer that they might be upheld until I should get out; but never was the arm of the Almighty so evidently uncovered before my eyes, as when passing down this valley.

The impression upon every thoughtful mind is deep. Sometimes it is overpowering. On the trail toward Gentry's, later in the day, I met two men from Illinois, on their way down. They succeeded in getting up as far as Hutchings'. After remaining an hour, they turned about, and came directly back, the same afternoon. When asked why, they said, they could not explain it, only that the impression upon their minds was insupportable. They appeared to be intelligent men.

On the south side of the valley, a half mile below "El Capitan," like a scarf of white lace, hanging from the shoulder of a goddess, is the "Bridal Veil." The fall is nine hundred feet. The wind blowing up the valley, swayed it to and fro, while rainbows hung in its graceful folds.

I went slowly up the miserable trail, on the north side, toward Gentry's, often looking back to catch another parting view of "Yosemite"—the "Great Grizzly Bear." The Indian name is the more beautiful, "Ah-wah-nee."

I met several parties on their way down. Some, to see the valley; others, in honor of their noble country's birth, to chase the greased pig.

Some were enthusiastic as they were dusty. Others were disgusted with the wretched trail, the poor beasts, and the poorer saddles on which they rode.

Among others I met, were two young gentlemen, as sprucely dressed as divinity students. They looked quite professional. We mutually halted, though our horses were at an angle of nearly forty-five degrees.

" How far yet to the bottom?"

" About three-quarters of a mile."

" Three-quarters of a mile! What a confounded set of liars! They told us at Gentry's that it was only three miles to the foot of the trail, and I am sure we have come *five* already."

" A new road like this seems long."

As they slid on down among the dust and loose stones, I heard some additional language that convinced me, they were not paying much attention to divinity.

The impressions of " Yosemite " can never

be forgotten. It is a valley "*sui generis.*" Even without the awful framework in which it is set, the place is a gem of rare beauty in itself. The "Merced" is as pure as opaline crystal. The magnificent trees upon its banks, the evergreens, and the level meadows on either hand, make it a beautiful place in which to live. The climate is enjoyable the whole year round. There is some good stock in the pastures, the roads and bridges are in good order, and the houses and hotels are credit· able structures.

The whole valley is set apart by National and State authority, and is under control of a Superintendent. No one is allowed to mar the natural scenery, either by chopping down the trees, or that worse modern vice, painting advertisements on the rocks. Here is, at last, one spot on earth, where the tourist can see the works of God without being compelled, at the same time, to take patent medicine.

Many persons go in there, in the early summer, and camp. At the date I was there, their stock had eaten up nearly all the grass, excepting what was enclosed in fields. For a gun, there is but little use. For the rod and line, unceasing employment.

In wild and rugged scenery, the Sierra Nevadas, about the head waters of Kaweah and Kings Rivers, excel "Yosemite." But for magnificent domes and unbroken granite walls, "Yosemite" is in advance of all the known world beside. While in some California wonders, I had been disappointed, in "Yosemite" I was not. It was more than had been told. And so, simply, because words are not adequate to the task. Making due allowance for all the discomforts of travel both by sea and land, I should nevertheless say, that it is well worth a journey of three thousand miles, to spend one hour upon "Glacier Point." And it is worth an equal journey, to stand below and look up at "El Capitan." They who have had the privilege ought to be both humbler and bolder, wiser and better.

CHAPTER VII.

THE GEYSERS.

FROM Yosemite via Garrote, Chinese Camp, Knight's Ferry, Stockton, San Francisco, Petaluma, and Healdsburg to "The Geysers," is three hundred and fifty-two miles. I reached Garrote on Friday evening, July 4th. The gentleman at my side, at supper table, proved to be the Sunday-school Superintendent. Our conversation developed my own occupation, and he gave me a pressing invitation to remain over Saturday and Sunday. The place had once been a flourishing mining town. They had an excellent school-house, and formerly, regular preaching. Now, the quartz mills were going to ruin, most of the mines were deserted, and the majority of the people had moved away. They had preaching only occasionally, as some bold itinerant

Methodist, or Cumberland Presbyterian, would come up into the mountains, and give them a sermon; and the Sunday-school was all they had left.

Most of the remaining population was Roman Catholic. A priest came around regularly to look after them, but the community had no confidence in his piety. They could scarcely be expected to have, for just on the previous evening, he rode through the village intoxicated, and when he came to the fork of the road, his horse bore to the right, he kept ahead, and fell helpless into the road. Then his people had to look after him. And the like had frequently occurred before.

At a later hour I met Mr. Foote, the gentlemanly proprietor of the hotel, and also his excellent family. I consented to remain. The Sunday-school numbered about thirty. They were bright and orderly. None of the officers were professors of religion, but they believed in the Sunday-school, and kept it up for the sake of their children. I made a brief address. The majority remained for service, and a very few others gathered in. As there was no physician present to forbid me, I preached as an experiment, for the first time in nineteen months. The little company heard attentively, while the preacher once more enjoyed the privilege of proclaiming to men, "Ho, every one that thirsteth, come ye to the waters, and he that hath no money; come ye, buy, and eat; yea, come, buy wine and milk without money and without price." Is. lv. 1. The day passed most pleasantly with that kind, warm-hearted people.

But this seems to have little to do with "The Geysers." However it may be to the reader, to the writer, a Sunday and a Sunday-school in such a rough ·mountain village, are far sweeter than the sulphurous fumes from the crater of a slumbering volcano. To make up for lost time, we will take a leap of three hundred miles, and alight upon the new stage-road above Healdsburg. It is a good piece of work, and there is some fine driving done on it. Although the summit of the highest mountain crossed is three thousand two hundred feet high, yet the grade is so easy, and the road way so smooth, that they pass over it in a sharp trot, and some parts at full gallop. There are thirty-five sharp turns in the road, and along-side, some fearful precipices where there is not a foot to spare. The morning stage came up behind me in the mountain. I had barely time, by spurring forward, to get to a place wide enough to let it pass. The driving was frightful. They say, however, that accidents seldom occur. Their harness, vehicles, and drivers, are all first-class, and the saying, "As poor as a stage horse," would be without point in California.

Yet, as I rode on, I could not help looking down into the fearful ravines, expecting to find them dashed to pieces. I was the more sensitive, as in coming down from Yosemite, a few miles below Hodgeson's, I saw the wreck of a stage that had upset only the day before. There were twelve passengers. Markley, an old and skillful driver, held the reins. Coming down an easy grade at a sharp trot, the leaders shied at a lunch paper lying against the bank.

In a moment, stage, horses, and all, were rolling over and over down the hill. Fortunately
the hill was not steep, nor were there any
rocks or large trees close to the road. The
top broke clear off the stage, at the first revolution, and the whole mass of passengers remained in it, about fifty feet from the road.
The body and running gear went a full hundred feet further, and, with the team, were
stopped by a big oak tree. Of all the passengers not a bone was broken. I saw some of
them both at Hodgeson's and Garrote. They
were bruised—some of them severely—and
were unable to tell how it was that they were
not all killed. One of them, limping around
on a stick, used bitter language, and seemed
to be sorry that they were not.

But about "The Geysers." Pluton Creek
flows from "The Geysers," westward, and emp-
ties into Russian River, just north of Cloverdale. Embowered among trees, the hotel at
"The Geysers" stands upon the south bank of
the creek. The spot is a charming one in itself.
Just opposite, opening in from the north,

almost at right angles to Pluton, is "Geyser Canyon." The hill in which it is cleft is probably fifteen hundred feet high. The canyon, or *ravine* more properly, is scarce a half mile long, the sides are irregular, very steep, and almost wholly without vegetation. The earth composing them looks like a mixture of brick-dust and sulphur. Volumes of steam constantly issue from it.

After crossing the foot-bridge over Pluton Creek, you find two trails, one to the left, entering the canyon from below, the other to the right, passing around the outer rim and entering at the upper end. I took the latter. To the right of the steep ascent are hot sulphur springs, the water from some of which is conducted into little bath-houses, where those wishing it can get either a vapor or shower bath. A little higher up, the spongy earth is full of sulphur and other suspicious minerals. Further on, the abundant contents are literally boiling over, the ground is hot and tremulous, steam is hissing through, and beautiful crystals of pure sulphur are hanging about the seething vents.

Descending into the ravine, and looking downward, you get a very impressive view. Nor is the *view* one-half of the whole. You hear sounds the most ominous, and smell odors the most villainous. Right here, in the exalted center, is an eminence about fifteen feet high. It is composed of sulphurous earth, and you recognize it at once as "The Devil's Pulpit." Probably considering the fact that the owner has a good deal of interest in this country, somebody had planted upon it a rough pole, bearing a tattered specimen of the American flag. Without any invitation from the presiding genius, I mounted the "Pulpit" and surveyed the surroundings. They are emphatically *infernal*. All around were piles of sulphur and other chemicals. Some mixed with earth, some in crystals, some in solution, and others flying off in vapor. Away down below was the "Witches' Caldron." There was evidently a big fire under it. The

> " Eye of newt and toe of frog,
>
> Wool of bat and tongue of dog,
>
> Adder's fork and blind-worm's sting,
>
> Lizard's leg and owlet's wing,"

were all in, and violently cooking. It was easy to join in the chorus,

> "Double, double, toil and trouble—
>
> Fire burn and boiler bubble."

Down there, also, were the "Devil's Ink Bottle," and the "Devil's Apothecary Shop." The supply and variety of drugs were enormous. Amid all these horrible surroundings, the "Devil's Grist Mill" was blowing off steam, while on his pulpit, were a superannuated flag, and a supernumerary preacher.

Conscious of incapacity to fill such a pulpit, and do justice to the occasion, I hastened down, to more carefully see the sights, hear the sounds, and smell the smells. The latter, are so strong that you can readily *taste* them, too. I thrust my little thermometer, which registered only 130°, into one of the springs. The mercury struck the top of the tube in a moment. At another, I saw an apparatus on the end of a pole, for cooking eggs.

The greatest curiosity is in the east bank of the canyon. Here, at one place, are numerous vents and openings in the rocks and sulphurous earth. You hear a regular succession of heavy thumps, like the strokes of a large engine in an old rickety mill, feel the hot ground tremble under your feet, and see the fierce steam escaping and the regular pulsations of the water rising and falling in the holes. That there are enormous steam works just inside, there can be no doubt. They are known as "The Devil's Grist Mill." They seemed to be appropriately named, for the only meal made is flour of sulphur.

Seeing no hope of doing any good, as the place was wholly devoted to witches and his Satanic majesty, I hurried out of that "bad place," hoping never to see, hear or smell its like again.

Later in the day, in going westward toward Cloverdale, I found the north hill-side a mile below "Geyser Canyon" of the same volcanic formation. Both to the practical Chemist and to the Geologist, a visit to the place would be of much more than ordinary interest. To the unprofessional, it is simply a great wonder, yet well worth a visit.

Eleven miles of the new stage-road from Cloverdale were then finished. By this nearly level road, it is now reached in two hours. The excitement and danger of the wild mountain ride, over the Healdsburg road, are exchanged for the shorter route.

CHAPTER VIII.

MENDOCINO County has a coast line of about one hundred miles. Extending inland, about sixty miles, to the Coast Range, it is about twice as large as the State of Delaware. It is heavily timbered, very mountainous, well watered, and abounds in fish and game. It contains several lakes, and some magnificent valleys, among which are Anderson, Round, Potter, Eden, Long, and Little Lake valleys. Near its centre is the dividing ridge between the Eel and Russian rivers, the former flowing northward, the latter toward the south. There are also numerous streams that empty into the Pacific within its own coast line. One of the largest of these is called Rio Grande, or "Big River."

Having a brother living in Little Lake

187

valley, I was on my way north, to spend a couple of months with him. To visit the Geysers added only about twenty miles to my ride, and on leaving them, I· finished the remainder of my journey in two days. Bill was tired enough, and so was his rider; but both were in good condition. Indeed, life in the saddle was becoming quite normal, and I once thought seriously of returning east by that mode of conveyance. Next to "travel afoot," it affords the best opportunity to know the country and its people. It is slow, but very satisfactory. The longest ride I made, in a day, was only about forty miles, which some good walkers would readily accomplish. Among rough mountain trails I found two-thirds of that distance quite sufficient. While company would be preferable, yet there are some advantages in travelling alone. On the much used roads and trails, dust is a very serious annoyance, both to stage and saddle-train. Alone, you have no dust but your own, and that can be avoided. Then when you are tired, the whole caravan is tired, and is willing to rest. When you want to go, the whole caravan wants to go, and there is no grumbling. My expenses averaged about three dollars a day, for self and horse.

At Stockton, I had tried to sell my horse and out-fit, intending to finish by river, rail, and coach. For excellent saddle, bridle, blankets, picket-rope and *horse*, the only dealer who would make me an offer at all, offered me the value of the saddle and blankets alone! There was no sale, and I was subsequently glad for my good, faithful horse.

Little Lake Valley is a gem. It is elliptical in form, about eight miles from north to south, and four from east to west. Heavy groves of oak are scattered through the valley, and numerous springs constitute the source of Eel river. Around, rise the mountains, from five hundred to two thousand feet high. Some are covered with manzanita and oak, others with pine, red-wood and fir. On some of the lower hills and pasture lands, the red trunks and brilliant green leaves of the *madroñne* add variety. They look like giant laurels.

One of my first expeditions was for mountain trout; but it was almost an utter failure.
My hook, line, pole, and hands were all too
unwieldly to take those active little sprites
from their crystal hiding places. At a ranch,
up among the hills, I got a thread, and made a
finer line. I then rigged a less hook on a
very small pole. A little bare-foot boy, who
understood the business, got his tackle, and
went with me down into the dark, rocky ravine. He could catch three to my one, though
I lost more bait than he. That there was high
art in fishing, dawned slowly upon my mind.

In my boyhood days, many were the long
strings of "red-fins," "sunnys," "chubs" and
"cat-fish" that I had taken from the old
Conestoga. These required a wholly different
treatment. Evening found me on my way
home, after travelling about six miles, a large
part of the way over rocks and among brush,
with a string of thirteen little trout, the largest
of which was not over seven inches.

Having learned a little by experience, I
made a line of fine black silk, twisted and

doubled. To this was attached a very small hook. A little pepper-wood rod, the size of a carriage whip, constituted the pole. Thus furnished, a company of us started early one morning, and drove six miles to Blosser's saw-mill, in a red-wood canyon. The stream was very low, but in places there were deep crystal pools, with drift-wood and huge red-wood logs in and around them. By going carefully, and slyly dropping the baited hook over a log, we caught a few. Mr. Blosser could catch them nearly as fast as he could throw in his hook. However, fortune favored me for once. Standing on a log, four or five feet in diameter, a portion of which was under water, I dropped my hook quietly down. A big fish-head reached out, took it, and withdrew. I thought, of course, he would soon break my little thread and get away, but concluded to worry him awhile. My line was only three feet long, and I just kept it gently stretched. He floundered about wildly, under the log. In five minutes, he showed signs of weariness. Tightening up on him gradually,

I led him out in sight. He was a splendid speckled trout. He soon became perfectly docile, and I led him along to shallow water, at the end of the pool, and caught him. He was nineteen inches long, and weighed two pounds.

In several pools, through this canyon, were a few salmon trout still larger. They seldom bite at a hook, and it is almost impossible to spear them, because of the depth of the water, and their secure hiding-places under the banks and projecting roots of trees. At certain times in the day, they come out and swim around, sometimes within a few inches of the surface. Then they may be shot with ball.

One day I accompanied Mr. Blosser, to try to secure some of them. "Betsy" had come by express, and, of course, she was along. Mr. Blosser had a little German rifle that carried a very large ball. Reaching the ground, we crept quietly through the bushes to the edge of the pool, where Mr. Blosser knew there were two. When we rose, side by side, with our guns cocked, there they were swimming around, as if taking their morning exercise. Splendid fellows they were, too, fully two feet long, one leading, the other following.

The water was clear as the sky, and they were a foot beneath the surface. Mr. Blosser said it was useless to shoot when they were lower than eight inches, and that it was very uncertain below six. While we conversed in whispers, they made another circuit and came nearer the surface. They were about five feet below us, and only fifteen distant. When they came opposite again, we each singled a fish, aimed well under, to allow both for the refraction of the light and for the reflection of the ball, counted "one," "two," and "bang" went both guns at once. The water flew, and when the smoke was gone, so were the fish. Really believing that we could not have annihilated them utterly, we loaded up again, and watched. In less than a half-hour, one came out. At Mr. Blosser's request, I tried again. The ball pierced him above the gills and nearly severed the head. He was twenty-six inches long, and weighed six and a half pounds.

13

Mr. Blosser knew where there were two more, a mile further up the canyon. We went, and had an interesting time.

Lengthwise, through the pool, lay an immense red-wood log, about two and a half feet of it above the water and as much beneath. The water, itself, was about four feet deep. We soon saw the fish hidden beneath the log and some drift. To shoot them was impossible. I thought they might be "hooked," as we hooked suckers, and for the purpose, rigged a large hook, with three or four inches of line, on the end of a four-foot stick. Mr. Blosser leisurely sat on the bank to see the sport. With my implement I got upon the log, and by lying down upon my stomach was able to look well down and under.

There one lay, not on the bottom, but suspended motionless within a few inches of the log, and directly under the centre of it. Some dead poles of drift-wood, lay from the bank to the log. To see and reach so far under, I was in need, either of weight to my heels, or support to my head. The former was not to

The "Parson" going down after the fish.

Page 195.

foot, but the latter, seemed to be at hand. So I put my left hand upon one of these poles, and with my fishing tackle in my right, projected my head and breast well over, feeling quite sure I should now catch him. But I didn't. Mr. Blosser heard a crack and a plunge, and saw a pair of shoes sticking above the water. Presently the shoes went down, and the other end of a man came up, who, by and by, reported, that he "went down after him, but didn't succeed." Then followed a divesting, wringing, and putting on of wet clothing, and a rapid walk down the canyon.

A dry, woolen shirt was borrowed, and no evil effects followed. The Methodist " Parson" was teased about turning Baptist. He steadfastly affirmed that he was, more than ever, opposed to immersion—especially head foremost, in cold spring water, and that without ceremony.

Subsequently, he went with Mr. Blosser again, for those same fish, and from that same log, caught them both with a heavy horsehair loop. Moreover, it should be said, that the brilliant success did not efface from his mind an important lesson in reference to leaning upon untried supports.

Mr. Blosser invited me to go with him on a four days' hunt. On the forenoon of Tuesday, August 5th, we started, with two horses hitched to a light spring wagon, went out on the Mendocino road seventeen miles, and camped on Big River. The whole surface of the country is made up of sharp and steep hills and mountains, separated by narrow ravines and canyons, and all covered with timber—mainly red-wood, fir, and sugar pine. We looked for game on the way, and in the evening, but saw none. Next morning, we took early breakfast, and then went in different directions. Both returned luckless. We harnessed up, drove on, and met a young man known as "Spanish George," in search of a stray horse. We gave him information about his horse, and he us about the best hunting ground. We went two miles further down the river, and camped again on a flat, among high grass and tar-weed. This latter is a terrible nuisance. It grows all heights, up to five feet, and is as sticky as its name indicates. The manes and tails of horses feeding among it, mat together like rough strands of tarred rope.

After dinner, we took to the hills, each alone. On returning to the river, I met "Spanish George." He had found his horse, and having his rifle and dog along, was going to take a little hunt, before going home. He invited me to go with him, and we took trail down the river. The red-woods had been cut off, a few years before, and a heavy growth of brush had taken their place. As we went quietly down the narrow trail, the dog followed close at the heels of the master, who glanced into the bushes right and left, on the alert for game. Suddenly, he raised his gun, fired, and told his dog to go. At the crack of his rifle, I saw a half grown deer leap from the grass, and bound into the brush. He had seen its ears, and fired as it jumped from its bed. The dog ran into the thicket, bayed, and scoured all around to the hill-side. I, too, went in and stood upon a large log. Presently, the dog raised it again, and here it came, bursting through the thicket, and running right toward me, alongside the log. I fired ball at its head, as it flew past the muzzle of my gun, and sent a charge of buck-shot after it, as it went into the thicket again, twenty feet away. A moment later, the dog was upon it, and George came up and secured it. Having hung it up, we went on down the river. I tarried behind, after awhile. As George and the dog went on, over some rough ground, I heard to their right a little noise, and immediately ran back to clear ground. Two deer emerged upon the hill-side, and when I bleated, they paused. But only a moment, for before I could get "Betsy" upon either one, they slipped behind the big trees and were gone.

I then returned, to get Mr. Blosser to come down where deer seemed almost as plenty as cattle in a pasture. It was late when I found him, and as we went down again, we met George carrying a little fawn. Its cry was most mournful. He had shot the dam, before seeing the fawn, and seemed sorry for the little orphan. He was going to take it along home for a pet. We got no game, but George generously gave us some meat.

Next morning, when I went to the river to wash myself and get water, a deer ran up on the opposite side, and stood on the edge of the heavy timber. I went back for "Betsy," and when I returned, he had gone. Careful search failed to find "the other one." After breakfast, we both went down the river, one on either side, fully expecting to find game. Mr. Blosser saw a deer, but could not get a shot. Three miles below, we met, and returned together. Luckless still, we got back before noon, harnessed up, and returned up the river toward our former camp. We sat, side by side, on the front seat. As we passed through a flat, Mr. Blosser stopped the team, put on the brake, gave me the reins, and showed me a deer directly to our left, about one hundred yards away. He had his head behind a bush, but his body was all exposed, and he presented a fair broadside. Mr. Blosser rested his rifle on my back, took a deliberate aim, and fired. The deer bounded into the brush. We tied the horses, and went in. Two ran out and sped up the hill-side. One of them was a fine buck. "Betsy" sent two loads of buck-shot after him, at about one hundred yards. He simply switched his tail in acknowledgment of the attention, and continued on his way. I then feared that one of them had been Mr. Blosser's target. But he was sure he had shot him through the body, just behind the shoulder. And further search proved him correct; for the deer jumped from the brush, and started up the hill. From a large log, Mr. Blosser sent another ball, at about sixty paces. Pierced again, he sprang forward and fell. He was a splendid buck. The first ball had struck him two inches too far back to cause instant death. We went on up, and camped at the forks of the river. It was three o'clock when we prepared and ate dinner. Roast venison, of our own killing, was refreshing.

Up one of the forks, directly eastward, Mr. Blosser knew there was a dam, below which was a hole, said to contain fish. It was three miles; but we concluded to go. There might be game, too. We went afoot. Most of the trail was very good, but part of it impassable for a horse, on account of the numerous logs cut the previous season.

On the way, we saw a few speckled trout, in the then feeble stream, but no game. Arrived at the dam, we found a hole about ten by twenty feet, made by the water that had rushed through the sluice-way. The water was perfectly clear, and about six feet deep. On one side, there was perpendicular rock, on the other, there were rocks and a large tree, beneath the roots of which was a hiding-place, extending backward and downward, at least two yards. When we came up, there were eight or ten fine salmon trout swimming around. Like frightened birds, they fled to cover. After awhile, one came out, and I fired at it a useless load of buck-shot.

It was night when we got back to camp.

Next morning, Mr. Blosser took both horses, and went down stream to hunt. I determined to try those fish again, took fresh venison for bait, plenty of large hooks, horse-hair for loops, "Betsy" and bullets, and thus equipped, travelled up the canyon. Moreover, my full assurance of *fish*, was evidenced by an empty sack, slung around my shoulders.

At 7½ o'clock, I had a large hook baited and in. One soon came out, and boldly took it. Then there was a "taut" line, a bending pole, and lively play. Far beneath the bank, and anon, to the opposite side, lengthwise and diagonally, he darted through the pool, like a gleaming shuttle. In a few minutes, I led him out to shallow water, and secured him. Then I sat behind the tree, and watched and waited a long time, in vain. When the fright had subsided, they would come cautiously out in turn, and nose the bait, but not lay hold. At last one took it, the fisherman's thrill again seized me, as his struggles began to pulse along line and pole, but, unlucky moment, he let go! It was no use. They would come out and scornfully swim past my tantalizing bait. One fine fellow persisted in making his circuits around the pool. For him, especially, I took over thirty horse-hairs, plaited a loop, and fixed it securely to the end of a five-foot rod. As he came sweeping around, about a foot beneath the surface, leisurely revolving in his elliptical orbit, I gently lowered before him. Not liking to pass through a five-inch ring like that, he turned aside, made another revolution, and at the same low velocity, came round again. He seemed less annoyed by my interference, but again dodged my trap. The third time, when he turned to the right, I drew it before him, and when to the left, by a quicker motion, I kept it before him still. He went in. When I thought he was far enough, I drew, and raised him to the surface. Then he felt as heavy as a dog, began to kick for life, and slipped through the loop to the tail.

With both hands, I pulled him out, and up on the rocks, four or five feet from the water, he all the time kicking like a crazy pig. Letting go my rod to lay hold of him, he jumped out of my hands, kept on jumping, and in a moment, was in the pool, and back in the hiding-place. He showed marked dislike to the new element, and to the formation of new acquaintances. Myself, and the rocks around, were wet enough to have been in a shower.

It was my first wrestling match with a fish, and his strength and agility proved more than a match for me. Another hour's patience brought out another fish, about the same size. "Betsy" paid careful attention to him, and when his unfortunate head came near the surface, she put an ounce of lead through it. Having no hope of another, soon, and the two I had weighing about ten pounds, without their heads, I sacked them, and started for camp.

From a little flat, among heavy timber and brush, three deer started up the mountain side. One paused; his position was unfavorable, but I fired, and thought I wounded him. Loading and going up the hill in pursuit, I saw another standing under the end of a huge burnt out log. He was a young buck, stood broadside, and leisurely eyed me. I was only sixty paces away, but too much excited to take steady aim. Intending to fire one barrel only, I discharged both. He plunged forward, fell almost to the ground, and then staggered into the brush. I loaded, went in, and expected soon to find him. I followed his track, then lost it, spent an hour in vain search, and then, thoroughly disgusted with my miserable shooting, took up my fish again, and trudged back to camp. After curing my fish, I ate a lunch, rolled up in a blanket, under the wagon, and went to sleep.

After awhile, Mr. Blosser returned with one small deer. We harnessed up and started homeward, sharply looking for game on the way. Mr. Blosser kindly offered, that if I saw a deer, I should shoot it with his rifle. As we were toiling up a long grade, I saw one. It stood off to our left, across a deep ravine, only seventy or eighty yards away. The wagon was stopped. I sat still, rested my elbow upon my knee, took deliberate aim, and fired.

The deer leaped forward, and fell among the bushes.

" Well done for you! you saved him," said Mr. Blosser. While he re-loaded, I took "Betsy," ran around the head of the ravine, and went into the brush to find and despatch it. When I got within a few paces, it got up, staggered along the hill-side, but kept out of my way, and most of the time, out of my sight. The thick underbrush prevented shooting again, and I tracked it by its blood. Once I was almost upon it, when it jumped from its bloody bed, and rushed through the bushes. A load of buck-shot turned its course down into the canyon. Mr. Blosser came, and we followed it a full half mile, raised it twice in the pursuit, headed it off once, when it took to the opposite hill, and then we were compelled to give it up. I could have wept for the poor beast, doomed, doubtless, to die after protracted suffering.

We camped along the road at a spring, and next morning drove home. Mr. Blosser had killed all the game. I had nothing to show but fish, and they were not so heavy to carry as was the remembrance of those wounded deer. I resolved to practice with my brother's rifle, and use it next time. At a target, there was no trouble, but I found a vast difference between coolly firing at a target and shooting at large game, that starts up suddenly. Old hunters become used to it. I found that all amateurs had an experience very similar to my own—often missing, and always crippling more than they kill. Some always use a dog. "Spanish George" never went without his, and he would probably have got neither of the two, the time I was with him, had it not been for his dog. Similar help would have secured both of my cripples.

I heard of a man in Mendocino, who thought a dog so essential, that on one occasion, when a fine buck came and stood in the woods in full view, just back of the house, he took down his gun, and then stepped front to loose his dog. When he returned, and sighted around the door jamb, there was nothing but trees! They often do stand a long time, and gaze in perfect simplicity.

In Tulare, Mr. Carter's two children were going a few miles to a neighbor's. Only twenty paces from them, they saw a deer; and he saw them. One remained to watch, the other went home to get her father. He took down the rifle, and went in bright anticipation of fresh venison. When he came to the place, there stood the deer, as intently watching the little boy as the boy was watching him. The father drew up, took good aim, and pulled. The cap burst without discharging the gun. The spell was broken. The deer tossed back his antlers, and dashed away like the wind. When I passed in the evening, the old man told me about it, introducing the story by saying, "I had bad luck to day." And I suppose he spoke the truth, for he was out of meat, and not to have good luck, under such circumstances, is *positively bad.*

By practicing on the heads of hare, at from forty to sixty paces, I acquired a little skill in the use of the rifle. I went hunting one day, with Mr. Sawyer, a neighbor. We took a horse to pack our game, and went up into the mountains, on the south-west side of the valley. In the forenoon, we both saw deer, and fired at them, but at such long range that it was almost hopeless. With us, it proved entirely so. Toward evening, we hunted awhile together. Three bounded up. Two plunged into the bushes, and one stood looking at us, only fifty yards away. We fired together. It simply whirled around and stood again, on the quarter. While we loaded, it seemed fixed, looking at us. First ready, I fired again. It whirled into the brush. Mr. Sawyer told his dog to go. It had fallen, but the dog raised it, and both went at a dreadful rate down the brushy ravine. The dog bayed, Mr. Sawyer followed, and as soon as "Betsy" was ready, the "parson" "came tumbling after."

The dog overtook it, or it had fallen after running about three hundred yards. The ball had entered just back of the shoulder blade, had pierced the lungs, and gone entirely through the body. One of the first shots had

14

simply cut the skin on the top of its neck.
The "tug of war" was now at hand, viz: to
get that disemboweled, headless, legless trunk
to the trail, at the top of that fearful hill.   One
took both rifles, the other the carcass.   Then
there was slipping backward, holding to roots
and bushes, and sweating slowly upward.
After several changes, we reached the trail
and the horse.   We concluded that hunting
for a living would be the hardest kind of work,
and in our case, very poor pay.

After adding another to my long list of
crippled deer, when on a trip to the coast, at
Mendocino city, I subsequently killed a yearling fawn, above Mr. Blosser's mill.   He had
shot the dam, and while loading, the fawn
came out of the bushes.   He fired, and was
quite sure he had killed it.   But night was
coming on, and he failed to find it.   Hunting
near the same place, a few days afterward, I
passed through a little opening in the timber
and brush.   A dead twig cracked off in the
woods.   I looked, and there was the beautiful
little animal about seventy yards away.   It

bleated and came trotting toward me. At thirty yards it stood. The cruel hunter raised his rifle and fired. It turned and ran into the brush. After re-loading, he followed in and found it dead. It dressed twenty-three pounds of excellent meat.

Beside hare and rabbits, there is plenty of other small game in Little Lake Valley. The "digger" squirrels are numerous, and in some of the groves, there are plenty of gray squirrels. Then the quail are often so abundant as to constitute a nuisance. About the last of August, the wild pigeons came in, too. "Betsy" and I secured a number of them. They are rather larger than the wild pigeons, east, and the young ones are excellent eating.

The climate is a curiosity. Frosts occur in mid-summer, while the morning sun that melts it, at noon, raises the mercury to 100°, in the shade. On Friday, July 25th, the thermometer ranged as follows: Morning 57°, noon 104°. On Saturday, the 26th, morning 57°, noon 107°. Sunday, 27th, morning 54°, noon 109°! About 11 o'clock, daily, a strong breeze sets in from the coast, and continues until the middle of the afternoon. This renders the heat quite endurable, and sunstroke seldom occurs.

There are no churches in the valley, but they have excellent schools; and the school houses are so commodious as to well serve a double purpose.

Like Goldsmith's useful piece of furniture—

"A bed by night, a chest of drawers by day,"—

so these well appointed houses. During the week, they echo the tread of bounding feet, the voice of the teacher, and hum of secular study. On Sunday, the arithmetic is brushed from the black-board, and the Scripture lesson substituted, and the Sunday-school joins in sacred song. At the teacher's desk, the preacher takes his stand, and instead of grammar, and history, and algebra, he talks "of Jesus and his love."

The Baptists and Presbyterians had preaching occasionally. The Methodists regularly, by a circuit preacher. I attended Sabbath-school, and was delighted to find both old and young taking an interest. It seemed impossible that such quiet orderly people could have so recently emerged from the rough ways of wild Californians. In the little grave yard, near one of the school houses, I saw the graves of five men, who fell in a fight on election day, a few years before. Two families had been involved in a quarrel, arising from a trivial cause, and they had settled it in that way. Armed with revolvers, ten took part in it, five on a side. They stood within a few paces of each other, and shot away, until the last man on one side fell. Seven were shot, but two recovered.

California life has developed a remarkable people. Or, perhaps, it would be nearer truth to say, sifted out a remarkable people. The very weak, and wholly bad, have mostly been swept away by the terrible ordeal through which all have passed. What the native born will do, remains to be seen. But of the sires, it may be said, that a sharper, sturdier, quieter, more obliging, and more sociable people, it would be difficult to find. For a lazy man,

or for a humbug, either in medicine, law, edu-
cation, or the pulpit, they have no use.

If a man has worth, either of muscle, brain,
or soul, they would divide their raiment to
keep him from suffering, and, if there was a
difference, they would retain the smaller half.
If he steals or worse, they just kill him.   Indeed, they have reduced life and death to a
money value, and they express it in financial
terms.   While dining at a hotel in San Francisco, a friend at my side, addressing another
gentleman opposite, alluded to the death, that
morning, of a man known to both of them.
In a most business like way, he replied:

"Yes, he has passed in his check."

On my brother's ranch, were the remains
of two Indian camps. The inhabitants had
been removed to a neighboring "reservation,"
though a few were still roaming about, and a
few had leave of absence to work during
harvest-time. Some of them are very good
hands—honest, steady, faithful. The labor on
many of the excellent roads, in the county,
has been done by Indians. Others are lazy,

drunken and worthless, just like white people.

They formerly lived mainly on roots and acorns; displaying great skill in catching fish, but none in taking game. The same seems to be true of nearly all the coast tribes. Acorns were abundant, and of these, they made a kind of coarse bread, that is nourishing. They dry, parch, and then pound them into meal. In Tulare County, along the Kaweah, and even away up in Grouse Valley, the holes are there in the granite rocks, in which they pulverized their acorns. On a flat rock, not more than ten by twenty feet, I saw more than a dozen. The largest was about ten inches in diameter, and nearly the same depth. Sometimes, within a few inches of a large hole, there was a little one, the size of a tea-cup, looking as though made by a child, working alongside of its mother. A man who engaged in the final raid upon those in Tulare, told me that the acorns they had stored that season, amounted to thousands of bushels.

On the "reservations," they are improving. Those in Round Valley are making commendable progress, under the instruction and care of Christian men. They have left off their heathen practices, have formed civilized habits, numbers of them have professed change of heart, and, judged by the result of tests to which all Christians are subjected, they give evidence that they both know, and experience what the Christian religion is.

The marked improvement in the condition of the Indians, on these coast reservations, is of itself, abundant proof of the wisdom of President Grant's policy toward these unfortunate wards of the nation. By the encroachments of white settlers, on the one hand, and by the stony hardness of unscrupulous politicians, pretending to furnish Government supplies, on the other, the Indians, for many years, had been ground as between two mill-stones. Not only mercy, but justice, as well, demands that these crushed remnants be treated as human beings. If the Sioux only, or Apaches are ungovernable, they alone should suffer for it.

CHAPTER IX.

SOUTHERN CALIFORNIA.

HAVING heard much of the "New Italy," as Southern California is called, I determined to take a trip to Los Angeles and Santa Barbara, before returning East.

For this purpose, I left Mendocino, returned to San Francisco, spent a few days attending the session of the California Conference, then meeting in the city, and on Monday, September 22d, at 9 A. M., sailed for San Pedro, in one of the Pacific Mail Company's steamers, plying between San Francisco and San Diego.

The boat was small, and we had only ninety passengers. Before reaching the "Golden Gate" we got into the fog, which prevails here almost constantly, at this season of the year. We ran close by the ill-starred "Costa Rica," which had run upon the rocks in the darkness, only a few nights before. I was glad we did not have to take her in tow again. Passing the "Gate," and heading southward, we found the fog more dense, and the sea rough for landsmen. Many of us were sea-sick, as usual, and the ordeal was passed, with all the grace possible, under the circumstances.

The boat was to touch at San Simeon, one hundred and sixty miles down the coast. At mid-night, the officers calculated we were in the neighborhood. Then commenced a protracted search. The whistle of the steamer was to be answered by a gun or horn on shore. So they blew and listened, listened and blew; advanced, and blew, and listened. Then they crept cautiously toward shore, blew, and listened. Cruised down the coast, blowing and listening. Fearing some dangerous rocks, they had to keep pretty well off. Daylight came. Nothing visible but fog. They whistled, and whistled. It reminded one of a child lost in the woods, who, weary with running and calling, at last sits down and cries. Silence—awful silence—was the only reply. But tears and inactivity never find an exit from trouble. Our little boat stirred around, for there was great uncertainty about the clearing away of that "black forest" of fog. During seven solid hours more, they continued the search. At noon, the signal was answered by the report of a gun on shore. Patience triumphed, after twelve hours' probation. Some passengers went off in a boat toward an invisible strand, and like a spectre, it came floating quietly back, bearing one beside the rowers.

The next point was San Luis Obispo. We got into the neighborhood at 5 P. M. Here the same process was repeated, but favorable results were reached, at the end of two hours and a half.

This whole southern coast is consecrated to the Saints. But we concluded that if they were all befogged as badly as Simeon and Luis Obispo, they would be poor aid to anyone in distress.

The next morning we were off Point Conception. The fog lifted. We got a view of the light-house, and heard the powerful fog-whistle. We now had grand sailing. The gulls and ducks sported on the water, and flocks of the huge albatross swept close to the surface of the smooth sea. Our course was nearly due east. The sky was cloudless. Far off to the right, were the large islands of Santa Rosa and Santa Cruz. Inland, and running parallel with the coast, were the mountains of Santa Inez. Saints to the right of us; Saints to the left of us; Saints in front of us! Pity there were not more in the midst of us.

At 1, P. M., we reached Santa Barbara. It took three hours to exchange freight. This allowed us a stroll upon shore. The situation of the city is very beautiful. It is nearly sur-rounded by mountains on the west, north, and east. The enclosed space is about three miles from north to south, by five or six from east to west. The rise from the beach is gradual. The streets cross at right angles and are well shaded, the favorite being the pepper tree. This tree has the strength of the maple, and yet, with its long compound leaves and slightly pendent branches, it has the charming grace of the weeping willow. Many of them were quite full of pepper berries, which were then turning from green to pink. The dense green of the orange and lemon, the broad and luxuriant fig in the gardens and orchards, and the great variety of ornamental flowers in the tastefully arranged door-yards, throw a charm about the whole place. Neat cottages, active business places, and some new and large hotels, indicate a fresh life in this old Spanish town. Facing the main street, leading up from the wharf, and just two miles from it, rises the low fort-like form of the old mission. The massive white adobe walls, pierced by little windows, that in the distance look like port-holes in a fortress, and the heavy tile roof, make it look as though wholly on the defensive. It is one hundred and fifty feet above tide, and visible far out at sea. Those devoted old Spaniards showed great, good sense in the location of their mission buildings.

The signal gun brought all the strollers on

board again, and we bade good-bye to the good lady Barbara. In the protected bay, are growing some gigantic sea-weeds, appearing to be attached to the bottom, five or six fathoms below. From central points they send up long vines, bearing an ovate leaf. The color is a greenish brown. These often reach the surface, and spread out ten or fifteen feet. Their motions were exceedingly graceful, as with the waves they were rolled back from our bow. But the side wheels made havoc among their fine forms, gathering and whirling them around by cart loads.

At 4½ o'clock, on Thursday morning, we were waked for breakfast, as the steamer entered the little harbor of San Pedro. San Pedro signifies "Saint Peter." This one, less fortunate than Peter of old, when sinking, seems to have had no saviour near, to lift it above the waves. There are only a few deserted walls of the old town yet standing. The harbor is being improved by the United States government, and the new town, three miles up the creek, is called Wilmington. They are trying to solve the problem of making a good harbor here, by means of a "break-water." The surroundings do not look en-couraging. Indeed, the whole sea coast of California, though it extends about eight hundred miles, furnishes only two good har-bors. But, as if to compensate in quality for the small quantity, these two are among the best in the world. They are San Francisco and San Diego.

The freight was transferred to a lighter, and the passengers to a little flat-bottomed steamer, that served the double purpose of tug and passenger-boat. We steamed for Wilmington. The creek, or slough rather, is equal in crookedness to the Christiana, below Wilmington, Delaware, while its depth is not nearly so great.

At Wilmington, we took cars. The distance to Los Angeles is twenty miles, nearly due north. The grade is ten feet to the mile, and the whole surrounding country has the same slope from the mountains to the sea. To the eye, it looks like a level plain. Ten miles out,

we reach Compton. It is a new town, looks
well on paper, fair to the eye in passing
through, and will very likely fulfill its great
promises.

Five miles further, Florence, younger yet
than Compton. There was very little but
stakes, marking the corners of town lots and
prospective fruit farms. But with such a site,
such a soil, and such a sun, with water from
the mountains, or a few artesian wells, will
produce a bearing orchard, or a populous
town, in a very few years.

Done with the saints, we have at last come
to "The Angels"—Los Angeles. After a
good dinner at the Bella Union, I found some
gentlemen to whom the "Masonry" of Method-
ism had given me an introduction. They had
the orthodox Wesleyan grip. A ride of fourteen miles around the country, was a real
luxury. The tons of ripe grapes, hanging in
two, three, and four-pound bunches, in scores
of vineyards, the live hedges, the fig orchards,
the wide spreading English walnuts, the emerald orange-groves, the crystal streams flow-

ing among them, and out in the country, the
fresher artesian wells, broad fields, where in
June a heavy harvest of wheat or barley had
been gathered, now covered with corn almost
ripe, that would yield over one hundred
bushels per acre, a cloudless day, and an atmosphere just sufficiently moist and comfort-
ably cooled, by the good breeze from the sea,
all conspired to remind one of Paradise re-
gained. The orange-groves, especially, present
a sight that sinks deep into the soul.

But a visit to the fine new school-house on
the hill, and a view of the Spanish part of the
town, known as Sonora, and more particularly,
a stroll through its dirty streets, and a glance
into its drinking and gambling saloons, filled
with half-breeds and greasy Mexicans, soon
dispel all hastily formed conclusions about
Paradise, and the already arrived Millennium.

Feeling thoroughly interested in this Southern country, I determined to go over to San
Bernardino, before turning around. It was
only sixty miles by stage, nearly due east.
We left next morning at 6.30. The horses
15

and stage were good, and we had a pleasant company of eight passengers. The hills soon enclosed us. Twelve miles out, we reached the old mission of San Gabriel. From the saints to the angels, from the angels to the arch-angel! Surely we must be nearing heaven.

Alas! appearances are against it. The old mission buildings are used for storage, stock, farming, and wine making purposes. Many of them are going into decay. Fifteen miles out, we change horses. Four fresh teams, of four each, are used in making the sixty miles. Forty miles out, we passed Cucamonga, where the wine, bearing that name, is made.

Here, they have immense vineyards, and the Indians had just commenced gathering the grapes. Scores of empty tierces were lying scattered in a grove near the wine press. A cooper was tightening them up, to hold the "Mocker." In regard to this business of wine making in California, it may here be said, that I asked the opinion of men in different parts of the State. Many of the people, including nearly all engaged in the business, not only justify it, but declare it an advantage to the country, in various ways.

But the great majority, not only of the Christian, but also of the thoughtful and observant people, who make no profession of religion whatever, as positively affirm, that it is proving an unmitigated curse. Vineyards of choice wine grapes are, yearly, being up-rooted, and replaced by varieties that produce raisins.

Soon after leaving Cucamonga, we entered a desert, that extends nearly the whole way to San Bernardino. Chemise and sage brush, grease-wood, fields of cactus, sand and boulders cover the cheerless plain. With the exception of a shower, three weeks before, no rain of any consequence had fallen for three years.

To the north-east of us, lay a high range of mountains, while directly in front, and visible during the last twenty-five miles of our ride, rose the lofty summit of Mt. San Bernardino. It seemed as though we should drive out of the desert, right up against the base of the mountain.   But there was said to be, between us and it, a valley forty miles long, and twenty miles wide.   Where could it be?   We presently learned.   Having got through the seemingly interminable sage brush and sand, we began an easy descent.   Before us, lay a vast elliptical basin, the bottom of which was not less than six or seven hundred feet below the desert we had crossed.   Well defined fields, trees and houses nestled among them, began to appear.   Then we first realized the distance between us and the base of Mt. San Bernardino.   Of this mountain, there are two peaks.   The more southern is the taller, the rounder, and more barren.   It is eleven thousand feet high, is covered during a large part of the year with snow, and is familiarly known as "Old Grayback."   The other, being a sharper peak, is taken as the base for surveys, in Southern California, as Mt. Diablo is, in Central.   It is in latitude 38°, 8', north, the same as Columbia, South Carolina.

The present town of San Bernardino is on

the west side of the valley, and about twelve miles from its northern end. It is regularly laid out, is well shaded, and contains a fixed population of about one thousand. The old Spanish mission, is six miles further east. The Mormons built the greater part of the present town, and had from the Mexican Government, a grant of the larger part of the valley. They were summoned home, some twelve years ago, sold out at an immense sacrifice, and started for Salt Lake. When on the way, however, they received some unsatisfactory intelligence, and a great many of them came back. They renounced polygamy, live there still, and are an industrious and valuable part of the population. This place is a centre for the miners to the north and east, and is also the point of departure for those going to Arizona and New Mexico.

On Saturday, I rode twelve miles through the country, with a gentleman who had long resided in the place. Seriously crippled by accident, he now lived by lending money, and riding about for his health. To a business

man, the former is quite agreeable, at from
three to five per cent. per month, and to an
invalid, the latter certainly pleasing, when the
route always lies along shaded lanes, across
sparkling streams rushing down from the
mountains, and amid the verdure and fragrance
of orange-groves.

I met, also, the leading physician of the
place. To my great surprise and pleasure, he
proved to be an old school-mate.

Sabbath was a precious rest-day. I attended
two church services and a Sabbath-school.
To participate with the laborers, in both fields,
was a real joy.

On Monday morning, at 6.30, we started
again for Los Angeles. I had the out-side
seat, and found the air really cold. In a
meadow, just outside of town, there was what
looked very much like white frost. The
thermometer marked 52°. At noon, it frequently runs above 100°. Nor is that surprising, for the valley is in the form of a basin,
with a hot desert to the west, high mountains
to the north and east, and its inclination

directly toward the noon-day sun. Its numerous streams, springs, and artesian wells, develop a heavy vegetable growth, and render it wonderfully productive.

At Los Angeles, I purchased a ticket, by the coast line of stages, for San Francisco. The first day's drive is to Santa Barbara, one hundred and ten miles. However, I concluded to spend a day at San Beneventura, the county seat of San Beneventura County, seventy-eight miles west. It was only five o'clock, and not yet light, when we drove out of town. It was cold, the stage was nearly empty, and the horses were full of fire. I had secured the outside seat. Inside were two—an old Frenchman, and a bottle of whiskey. They seemed to enjoy each other's company, and had a merry time of it. But high happiness, especially that which springs from such a source, often suffers serious interruption. So in this case. When we were rolling over a wide plain, the off-wheel horse began to jump and kick. His heels flew nearly as high as the top of the stage. In a moment, the team was off in a run. The driver feared to put his foot upon the brake-bar, for the horse's wicked heels seemed to make that the chief objective point. It was a full mile to the hill. The plain was perfectly even, excepting the hundreds of mounds and holes, made by the "digger squirrels." The driver asked me to take his hat and whip. Whether purposely or not, I do not know, we swept out of the beaten road. Away we sped; the hair of the driver streaming in the wind, his teeth set, and reins "taut," I, for life, holding to the iron guard around the seat, the stage making fearful jumps over the mounds and into the holes, the old French-man and his whiskey bottle bouncing about, like pebbles in a child's rattle, and anon crying for mercy. I looked to see his hatless head come through the top of the stage. After describing a wide semi-circle, we returned to the road, the horses cooled to a trot, Jehu had his foot upon the brake-bar, and now used both his hat and whip.

By and by, he gave me a little sketch of that horse. "He is a curious fellow. That's his second caper of that kind. Sometimes, he refuses to go at all; generally, in town. He prefers the Main street, stops, and looks about to *read* the *signs*. When he comes to a Dutch sign, it takes him longer than usual to *spell it out*. It takes a heavy fall of timber to wake him up."

We reached Beneventura at 3.20,P. M. It lies right along the sea-side, and there are high hills immediately behind it, to the north. There is a small wharf at which schooners and other light craft unload without lighters. It is an old Spanish town, and the venerable mission buildings seem to be in pretty good repair. There are many Mexicans in the town and surrounding country.

Going out to call upon a gentleman whom I had met in San Francisco, among other curiosities, I saw one entirely new, viz: a "Bull-fight." It is an annual festival with them. They proceed as follows:

From the town people in various kinds of business, especially the saloon keepers, they secure subscriptions to purchase lumber.

With this they enclose a space about one hundred feet square. The fence is about five feet high—the boards being put on horizontally, with ample cracks for the children to peep through. They secure from the neighboring ranches a number of young bulls, the wilder the better, lasso them, and saw off the ends of their horns. The day having arrived, the crowd assembles, and one of the beasts is run into the enclosure. The Matadores, attired in their best clothes, and seated in their best saddles, upon their most nimble horses, and armed with pistols only, ride gaily in after him. The sport consists, not·in torturing or killing the bull, but in making him furious, and then so managing the horse as to avoid his charges. The beast they had in, when I passed, had too much wit to trouble himself, either about their tantalizing motions, their Spanish bravado, or the long red scarfs they flaunted in his face. Several of his predecessors had been turned out, and denounced by the hooting crowd as impregnable cowards. He was in a fair way to share the same condemnation.

His would-be tormentors displayed a patience and ingenuity worthy of a better cause. But they evidently believed with Doctor Whedon, that "there is both freedom to an act, and freedom from it," for when he did make a start at one of them, though only in a smart walk, both horse and rider gave him ample room.

That was the second afternoon, and no animal, either quadruped or biped, had yet been hurt. But the spectators seemed interested, and hopeful that some good thing would yet happen. And such a motley assemblage! Boys and men, women and children, infants in arms, Spaniards and Indians, negroes and half-breeds, with a sprinkling of Chinese, in all styles of dress, with all hues of skin, on the fence, sitting, hanging, peeping through, on piles of lumber, on wagons, in carriages, and on horseback. And yet with all the variety of age, color, and nationality, they did not number over five hundred in all.

The better class of Americans took no interest in it, whatever, and the brick-layers, only a square away, kept steadily on with their work.

On the hill, back of the town, is a small reservoir that supplies water. To lay their dust and put out fires, they need neither sprinkling-cart nor fire-engine, for the one hundred feet of head sends a fierce stream through the nozzle of a hose.

More than a hundred feet above the reservoir, on top of the hill, stands a high wooden cross. As we were going down, I had noticed it from the deck of the steamer, far out at sea. I walked up to it, and found that it was planted in a heap of stones, laid in good mortar. · From appearances, it had stood there many years.

These people have an easy way of holding up the cross. They evidently think the steeple of a church, the dome of a cathedral, or the summit of a hill, more capable of bearing it than they. The mountain is left to carry the cross, while they enjoy the luxury of a bull-fight or gambling saloon, at its base. They are like the man who, thinking evening devotions in a cold room, before retiring, to be a wearisome business, tacked a copy of his prayer to the bed-post, and as he hopped hastily in, was accustomed to say to the Lord: "Them's my sentiments." Roman Catholicism has done them no good. Their religion has no spirit, and only a ragged and beggarly form.

At 4, P. M., we took stage again. The mountains soon curve around to the south-west, and confine the road to the beach. Fortunately for us, the tide was out. Sometimes, the stage is lifted up bodily, and the horses have to swim. One of the drivers had nearly lost his life. He gave up the situation, saying bitterly, that he "had hired to drive a stage, and not to navigate a boat."

We reached Santa Barbara at 8.30, P. M., and stopped at the "Occidental." Santa Barbara is taking the lead of all these Southern towns. Being on the sea coast, its situation is, in some respects, more favorable than that of Los Angeles. The temperature and rainfall are about the same, but the atmosphere is slightly dryer at the latter place. While the thermometer sometimes reaches 100°, at midday, the nights are always cool, and the worst of their winter corresponds very nearly to the April weather of the Middle States. The influx of people, and especially of invalids, has been very great, during the last four years. As a consequence, the prices of real estate have advanced, from two to five hundred per cent. in the same time.

The next day's ride, was to San Luis Obispo, one hundred and fifteen miles. We left at 4.50, A. M., had a very agreeable company, splendid team, and good driver. The road lay among mountains, and over small plains. We got out, and walked three miles up the Santa Inez Mountain. It is a huge mass of red sand-stone rock. In many places, grooves were cut, to furnish foothold for the horses.

From the summit, we had a grand view of the plain beneath, and the calm Pacific, bearing an occasional sail, far in the distance.

Much of the country we passed through

was very poor, and fit only for sheep pasture. The hills were bare and brown. There were scattering groves of oak on the plains, and a few other kinds of trees along the now dry water-courses.

The Santa Inez River, which we followed many miles, had dwindled to a brook, and in many places disappeared in the sand. It was 10.30, P. M., when we drove into San Luis. Excepting by the moon, when we drove in, we saw very little of the place, for we were off again at 6.30, next morning. But from what we saw, I should take Luis Obispo to be one of the poorest saints on the coast. Lack of wealth, however, is not of itself, positive proof that there is lack of merit.

Twenty miles north, we reached the head of Salinas River, and Salinas Plains. The road was as level and as hard as a floor of oak. Eight miles per hour, were traversed by our lively wheels. On either hand were high mountains. To the left, the San Antonia, to the right, the Coast Range. Raising sheep appeared to be the chief business. At one-

and-a-half hours after midnight, we reached Soledad, having made one hundred and thirty miles. This terminated a stage ride of four hundred and seventy-five miles. The cars took us over the remaining one hundred, to San Francisco.

CHAPTER X.

O N Tuesday, October 10th, I purchased a ticket for Philadelphia, and on Wednesday morning, at 7 o'clock, left San Francisco amid the first showers of the coming winter rains.

The first eighty-three miles, to Lathrop, I had been over in going to Visalia. Here a branch of the Central Pacific Road turns into Southern California, and is now nearly completed to Los Angeles. The main trunk runs almost directly northward, toward Stockton and Sacramento.

At Lathrop, the chief object of interest to most travelers, appeared to be a fine young grizzly bear, about the size of the one now in the Philadelphia Zoological Garden. In a good cage with iron front, only a few feet

16   241

from the depot platform, he sleeps away the lazy hours, or sits up to catch nuts and fruit, which some one is nearly always ready to supply. He seems to be as much at home as a fat pig in a comfortable pen, is much neater in his attire, and excepting his suspicious claws, looks as though he would make a very companionable pet.

It was charming, to see the patience that, for a quarter of a minute, kept his jaws ajar awaiting a piece of apple, which a mischievous boy tossed several times before letting go. He simply shut his eyes and waited, as though it cost him less effort to hold his mouth open, than it did the boy to make the motions.

Sacramento is one hundred and thirty-five miles from San Francisco, is situated at the junction of the Sacramento and American rivers, and is the second city in the State.

In addition to the cars, good steamers also, run daily to San Francisco, and it is the centre of an immense inland trade. It has suffered greatly from fire and flood—especially the latter. But with wonderful energy, the people soon rebuild it better than before, and at the same time, strengthen the defenses against the destructive elements.

Here you are only fifty-six feet above sea-level. The whole surrounding country is a magnificent district for farming. The immense piles of grain sacks, lying in the fields, two months before, had nearly all disappeared; and none too soon, for the sky was overcast, and the first rains were at hand.

From Sacramento there is a steady ascent, but so gradual for twenty miles as not to be apparent to the eye. In twenty-two miles, to Rocklin, you rise only two hundred and thirteen feet. Here you are among the first foothills. The road now sweeps steadily upward, along the crest of the ridge dividing the North Fork of the American River, on the South, from a little stream called Bear River, on the North.

Thirty-two miles bring you to Colfax, and lift you toward the clouds three thousand one hundred and seventy-nine feet, making a grade of almost one hundred feet per mile.

This district once contained rich placer mines. The canyons, and gulches, and hillsides, show their rocky ribs and make much of the country look like the bleaching skeleton of some unfortunate animal, which a beast of prey had devoured, and from the bones of which, the vultures had stripped the very sinews and ligaments.

In a few places mining is still going on, and you occasionally see the long flumes that bring the water down from the higher mountain streams.

The view toward the Summit, is at no point equal in grandeur to that further south. From Yosemite northward, the whole range appears to be toned down. Remembering that "Sierra Nevada," originally signifies "Snowy Saw," and hence, "snow-covered mountain ridge," we may say that the *saw* is comparatively dull. Whether in this part, subjected to longer or severer use, or whether not so deeply notched in the beginning, may not be known. But one thing is certain, the teeth are neither so prominent nor so sharp, as they are two hundred miles further south.

Toward the valley the view steadily widens, and becomes very fine. There was no open car on our train, and the choicest position was on the rear platform of the rear car.

From Colfax to Summit is fifty-one miles, rising three thousand five hundred and ninety-two feet. You are now seven thousand and forty feet above the sea. Around is a wilderness of mountains, none seeming to especially out-top his fellows.

Night had set in when we swept around the perpendicular mountain side known as Cape Horn. It is more than a thousand feet to the bottom of the gorge below, and the gathering darkness apparently added to its depth.

Fourteen miles, down a grade of over one hundred feet to the mile, now bring you to Truckee. At this point you can take stage, and visit Lake Tahoe. It lies only fourteen miles to the south, and is one of the most beautiful sheets of water in the world. Itself more than five thousand feet above the sea, it is yet surrounded by mountains rising more than two thousand feet higher.

The Truckee River flows into it, but there is no visible outlet. Its surface is nearly always smooth as a mirror, and its waters are so clear that a silver dime or white pebble may be seen at the depth of a hundred feet. But to sportsmen, its chief attraction is found in its finny population. While on the coast, I read of a trout being caught there, that weighed *twenty-five* pounds!

To carry the rail-road across the mountains this far, required some of the boldest feats of engineering. Passing through the cuts, over the bridges, and along the abrupt mountain sides, will necessarily remind one of the almost insuperable obstacles in the way of those who first surveyed the route and located the road.

The construction, too, was equally difficult. Every mattock and shovel, every pound of powder, every spike and bolt, every chair and rail, had to be brought from New York. All were shipped via Cape Horn to San Francisco.

Nor were steep mountain sides, and deep gorges, and solid granite, the only obstacles. At these higher altitudes, snow falls in the winter, many feet deep. When building the road, the workmen often had to tunnel their way through snow and ice, to get at their work ; and since the road was completed, more than forty miles of the track have been covered with snow sheds. Nor are these mere light and fragile structures. Often subjected to the pressure of the avalanche, rushing down the mountain, they are built of heavy timber, and, excepting occasional openings for air and light, are covered with plank.

Fortunately, none of the sections are very long, and you get frequent views of the mountain scenery. But often it is vexing, to have a burst of beauty snatched from your eyes, just as you are beginning to appreciate it.

At some of the stations, you see huge snow-plows. They are made to plough through snow as high as the top of the smoke-stack. It is said to be an interesting sight to see two, four, or half a dozen engines behind one of these, pushing a ten-foot snow off the track.

As on ship-board, amid the billows of the ocean, you witness the power of man wrestling with the forces of nature—ribs of oak and of iron sustaining the blows of wave and tempest—so up here, amid these changeless billows of granite, amid storms, torrents, frost and avalanche, this huge thing of fiery life stretches its iron form in graceful curves, and daily sends along its precious freight of perishable merchandise and immortal men. It is a battle among the clouds, and often above them.

Thursday morning found us at Wadsworth, Nevada. The last of the mountains had been passed in the night. We were now in the great basin between the Rocky Mountains and the Sierras. We had also passed Reno, whence a railroad runs southward fifty-two miles to Virginia City. This is the land of silver, as California is of gold. The silver mines of Virginia City and surrounding region are the wonder of the financial world. Hundreds of thousands of dollars' worth of the precious ore are daily lifted from the deep shafts. Immense fortunes are lost and made in these mines. They are in the hands of stock companies, and their shares are bought and sold in the San Francisco stock exchange, as are the shares of railroad stock in our eastern cities.

At White Plains, we pass a little lake known as Mirage Lake, and not far behind it, Humboldt Lake. This receives the Humboldt river, along which the road now runs the whole way to Tulásco, a distance of two hundred and eighty-four miles.

The whole country looks as if it had once been the bottom of a sea, and in turn, the crater of a volcano. Brown, barren hills are the only mountains, and stunted bushes the only trees. A few of these, just along the water-courses, do struggle up to five or six inches in diameter. The Humboldt river itself, was then only a respectable creek. The earth is strongly impregnated with alkali, and for scores of miles, sage brush is the only thing living that seems to be at home.

There are said to be some lean, lank hare that manage in some inscrutable way to eke out a precarious existence. We saw none of them.

What a traveller said of a section of Arizona might also be applied to this.

At a hotel, the landlord asked his guest whether he would have "wild duck."

"What d'ye call it?"

"Wild duck."

"What is that?"

"Why, a kind of bird—a water-fowl."

"Did it have wings?"

"Yes, certainly."

"Then I don't want any. Anything that has wings and don't get out of a country like this, is'nt fit to eat."

Early on Friday morning, we passed Promontory Point. This place is eight hundred and thirty miles from San Francisco, and is rendered memorable by the union of the Central Pacific and Union Pacific roads. The former, through mountain and desert, had pushed eastward from San Francisco and

Sacramento as a base. The latter, westward from Omaha. It was here, in the presence of officers and workmen—Yankees from both coasts, Chinamen from China, and Irishmen from Erin—that on the 10th of May, 1869, the last rail was laid and the last spike driven that completed the iron band across the Continent. It is said, that the hammer used in driving the last spike, and the spike itself, were connected with the telegraph, and thus each blow was simultaneously signalled, in New York and San Francisco.

With lofty barren hills to the left, and a level plain around, we now sweep close around the north end of Great Salt Lake. A few water-fowl are visible on its silver surface. Forty-four miles bring us to Ogden. This is made the terminus of the Central Pacific road. It is four thousand three hundred and forty feet above the ocean, and eight hundred and eighty-two miles from San Francisco.

From here, southward, to Salt Lake City, is only thirty-seven miles by rail. Most travellers stop over a day, and visit Brigham Young's

Paradise. I had just seen enough of physical desert to fully satisfy me. Five hundred miles of alkali and sage brush were bad enough. To add a view of the moral desert at Salt Lake would have been too much. If truth be told, the bitterness of wormwood is sweetness itself, compared with the greater part of inner life at Salt Lake.

The city is situated on a plain sloping from the Wasatch mountains on the east, to Salt Lake on the west. As there is no rain, they are wholly dependent on irrigation. The water is brought from the mountains, and is conducted among the numerous little farms, and along all the streets of the city. It is under the control of officers, and is turned into the gardens and orchards under strict supervision.

The city is regularly laid out, and is embowered among beautiful trees, furnishing luxurious shade and excellent fruit. The tithes of all fruit and grain go into "the Lord's treasury"—which there means, the capacious bins of Brigham's store-house. Grown fat and immensely wealthy upon the hard earnings of the poor dupes who believe his teachings, he can well afford to augment his sanctity by supporting a score of wives, and raising three-score of children. But the Gentiles, as all not Mormons are called, have come in among them. There are now in their midst Christian Churches and political papers, that dare to teach correct morals and republican government. When death relaxes the hand of the hoary tyrant who now wields the iron scepter, the whole institution will probably crumble to pieces.

Thirteen miles east of Ogden, the road enters Weber Canyon. This is a cleft in the Wasatch range. The western extremity of the opening into this "bad place," is fitly styled the "Devil's Gate." You are glad to find an easy exit toward sunrise and Christian civilization. For many miles, the road winds along Weber River, crossing, and recrossing the swift current. There is one tunnel five hundred and fifty feet long, and beyond it, near the track, a very unexpected object, viz: a lone pine tree. When the surveyors had measured to this point, they found it just one thousand miles from Omaha. It is known as the "Thousand mile Tree," and is marked to that effect.

Two hours more carry us into Echo Canyon. Here, the perpendicular sandstone cliffs, on the north side, are some five hundred feet high, and are wrought into various fantastic forms. It would seem that these, like many others further south, in this same range of mountains, are the work of sand-storms. Whirlwinds, lifting tons of sharp sand in their giant arms, revolve them among these soft sandstone formations, and work them out into these curious shapes, as with a huge, elastic, universal drill. Here, as in the clouds, the imagination pictures the faces and forms of bird, and beast, and man, of tottering turret and lofty spire.

On some of the heights above, are old fortifications, where, it is said, the Mormons prepared to resist the passage of United States troops, in 1857. With plenty of rocks for ball, and an unlimited supply of gravitation for powder, they were in a position to do fearful mischief. But both powder and ball remained unused.

The canyon is narrow and crooked. The railroad crosses the creek thirty-one times in twenty-six miles. There is one tunnel over seven hundred feet long. The grade is a heavy one, and a funny story is told of an incident that occurred when the road was just built. Paddy Miles was foreman on a construction train of sixteen cars, carrying ties and rails down to Echo. Unobserved, the four rear cars became uncoupled, and were left behind on an easy grade. They were a half mile behind, when first seen, and just approaching the heavier grade, where it would be madness to await their coming. There were two Dutchmen on them, but they were sound asleep, and so the brakes were unused. An exciting chase down the canyon now began. The engineer blew his whistle, and the rocks on either side multiplied the sounds. But the Dutchmen slept. What was to be done? They would soon reach the end of the road, where a smash was inevitable. Paddy concluded that it would be better to lose four cars and two drowsy Dutchmen, than twelve cars, an engine, and probably some men who kept awake; and so he ordered his men to throw ties off his rear car, in order to obstruct the track. On they went, flying around curves and over the bridges, signaling the switch open at Echo City. There the train was run upon the siding. A crash was heard up the canyon. The obstructions had proved effectual. Gathering the forces, they went back to see the wreck, and exhume from the debris the mangled corpses of the poor Dutchmen. They found the wreck a horrible sight to behold—trucks and timbers, ties and rails, mingled in dread confusion. They found the Dutchmen, too. Tossed out by the first concussion, they had waked up in a dirt bank, had crawled out wondering what had happened, and were now sitting down, smoking their pipes, and calmly awaiting developments.

From this point on, you begin to look for the Rocky Mountains, of which old and young have heard so much, ever since the days of primary geography. Onward to Green River, there is a slight descent, and from there the rise is so gradual, and the horizon so clear of peaks that you conclude there must have been some mistake in giving names. True, there are some large rocks, some deep gorges, and some respectable hills; but nowhere to be seen, the ideal "Rocky Mountains." The country is an improvement upon that west of Salt Lake, but the hills were bare and brown, the streams feeble, and generally an air of dreary desolation reigning over all. There were occasionally visible, some specimens of antelope, and there are said to be elk and deer in the mountains. At Creston, are some more natural plantations of sage brush. You begin to dread a repetition of the Humboldt River country. To your left you pass a little sheet of water called Lake Como. It may be well to have a great name when there is not much beside. It is about a mile long, and half a mile in width. It is said to contain a curious species of amphibious animal, resembling a

17

cat-fish, with short legs. Not only at home in the water, it can make considerable excursions upon land, also. A similar species, called the Axolotl, is found in Mexico, and is esteemed as an article of food. This species belongs to the family of "*Sirenidae*," and is known to Naturalists as the "*Siredon*." They are a strange connecting link between the lizard and fish. More favored than the latter, when one pond or stream dries up, they can set out in search of another.

Water, for use on the road, is frequently supplied from artesian wells. One of the deepest is at Point of Rocks. It is a little over one thousand feet deep.

Bituminous coal is mined in a number of places. From Carbon, large quantities are shipped eastward, to supply the towns along the road. Some of it is carried as far as Omaha.

The country really improves as you continue to ascend. You see more antelopes. At first in the far distance, then some start up near the track, scamper away a hundred

yards, and then turn and look steadily at the
train. Sometimes there were a dozen or more
in a band, often only three or four. Once I
counted over thirty within rifle shot of each
other, and once there was a poor lone one far
out on the plain, with no mate in sight. They
appeared very timid, and it looked as easy for
them to run as for a bird to fly. Indeed, this
is their only mode of defense. They are said
to act strangely, when attacked by hunters.
They will come within range to look at a red
scarf flying upon the tip of a ramrod, and
often when one of a band is shot, the others,
instead of running away for safety, will simply
race around in a little circle, while another
and another fall victims to the rifle. Their
flesh is said to be excellent. They were once
numerous in the valley of the San Joaquin,
but are now seldom seen there.

At Sherman, you reach the highest point
on the road between the two oceans. The
altitude is eight thousand two hundred and
forty-eight feet above tide. The town is
named for General Sherman, and receives more

honor than it is likely to confer.   For, about
twenty-five frame houses, including two hotels
and one store, give a very doubtful prophecy
of any future magnificence as a city.   The
whole surrounding country looks dreary and
lonely.   You are above most of the busy
world, and yet, were it not for the accurate
instruments of the civil engineer, you would
not believe it.   The loneliness is scarcely re-
lieved by two snow-covered peaks in the distance.   The nearer one, lies to the south-west.
That is Long's Peak, and it is seventy miles
away.   The other, is directly south.   That is
Pike's Peak, and you can scarce believe that
one hundred and sixty-five miles lie between
it and yourself.

Fish and game are said to abound within a
few miles.

The thermometer never rises above 82°, in
the summer, but it falls as low as 30° below
zero, in the winter.

Snow seldom falls more than a few inches,
and then the wind carries it into the hollows
and depressions on the plains.   This often be-

comes a serious obstacle in the way of the cars. To prevent it, there are built many miles of snow fences. These are sometimes made of rocks and stones roughly piled up. But they are mostly constructed of boards, about ten inches wide, nailed on horizontally, with spaces between them. The posts are inclined at an angle of about sixty degrees and instead of being planted in the ground, they are secured to timbers lying upon the surface. In places particularly exposed, several lines of these movable fences, are placed one behind the other. They break the wind and form the snow into huge drifts, before it reaches the road.

Thirty-three miles from Sherman, you reach Cheyenne. Unconsciously, you have descended more than two thousand feet. Here, where on July 4th, 1867, there was but one house, there is now a thriving city of several thousand inhabitants. Substantial and beautiful buildings of brick, are rapidly taking the place of the first rude frames. An excellent court-house, handsome churches, superior schools, fine stores, two or three enterprising newspapers, and a good water supply, are some of the evidences of a spirit, that is destined to make this an important city at an early day.

It is a curious fact, that this place is just midway between Omaha and Ogden—five hundred and sixteen miles from each. For pasturage, the surrounding country is one of the best in the world. Immense herds of cattle are handled in this district.

Greeley and Denver City lie directly south, the former, fifty-five, the latter, one hundred and six miles, and are connected with this place by rail.

From Cheyenne to Omaha, the country is drained by the Platte River. Apparently boundless plains spread out on every side. Here countless numbers of buffalo, or more properly bison, roam at large, and formerly could sometimes be seen from the cars.

It was here that the Grand Duke Alexis, of Russia, demonstrated his prowess in hunting, when on a visit to this country a few years ago. It would seem that he was not likely to fare better than amateurs, in whose veins there runs no royal blood.

However distinguished the honor would have been, none of the dumb beasts took a special fancy to being killed by the hand that is one day to wield the scepter over all the Russias. But it is said, that an old hunter, known as "Buffalo Bill," being ashamed of the conduct of the animals, and taking compassion upon the Prince, caught a calf by the tail, and held on until the royal Nimrod rode up and shot it. Of course, all his subjects will ever remember that their mighty Czar, in his youthful days, slew a buffalo on the American plains. It will make a nice story for the little Russians to spell out in their "First Readers."

Late in the evening, we passed Prairie Dog City. For miles along the road, these little fellows have taken up claims. At this place, immense numbers have concentrated upon a few hundred acres, and form a densely populated town. With the dirt excavated from the

hole beneath, they build a mound a foot or
more high. This furnishes a convenient ob-
servatory. When out feeding, if alarmed,
they scamper to the mound, sit up upon their
haunches, and if they think the danger immi-
nent, like their squirrel cousins on the coast,
they give a little bark and dive down. A
miniature city, with live inhabitants of the
same people, constitutes one of the most interesting features of the Zoological Garden, in
Fairmount Park, Philadelphia.

At twelve o'clock, on Saturday night, we
reached North Platte. To avoid travel on
Sabbath, I stopped over twenty-four hours.
Around this place there spread the same unbroken plains. The grass for miles along the
railroad was all burnt, and long lines of fire
were visible far out on the horizon. Great
herds of cattle are fed in this region, and all
the men employed for many miles around,
turned out to fight the fire. Here it had
proved too strong for them, and was then reported to be burning forty-five miles away.

Sabbath was beautiful. I found the parsonage of the only church in town, made the acquaintance of the excellent pastor, and shared the services with him. Though he and his people bore a name differing from that of my own denomination, the partition dividing us was soon reduced to a shadow, and before the service closed, even the shadow was obliterated by the light from the same face that shone upon Peter, and James, and John on the mount.

The whole town was as quiet as a New England village; and though there were numerous boarders at the hotel, there was neither drinking seen, nor swearing heard. Though I had not seen a buffalo on the plains, I had the privilege of tasting one at the dinner table. It was excellent, and I regretted not having an opportunity like that enjoyed by Alexis.

On entering the car again at midnight, instead of finding everybody snoring away as usual, I was surprised to find general wakefulness, and one group, near where I secured a seat, in very earnest conversation. It ran as follows:

"If it had been me, I would have put a bul-
let through him, as sure as fate," said a big,
determined man.

"No, you wouldn't," said a quiet, cool man.

"Yes, I would," affirmed the first.

"You would have done no such thing. No
man in his senses would have done so," declared the second.

"I would have shot one of them, at any
rate," said the first, driving his assertion into
the back of the seat before him with his fist.

"Well, suppose you had, where would you
have been? The others would have stuck a
knife into you, and dragged you out at the
back door, and you would never have been
heard from. Those fellows are prepared for
the worst."

Of the gentleman at my side, I inquired
what had happened.

"Oh," said he, "that man back there near
the door, was robbed at Sidney, when the
train stopped for supper. After the train had
been standing awhile, he went to the car door,
and was looking around for a place 'to get a

drink.' A gentleman on the platform said he could show him a place, as he was acquainted there. They went together, across the little open square, to a saloon. His friend soon got into a genial conversation with the bar-keeper. A throw at dice was proposed and accepted. His friend lost, and was not able to make change. He was courteously asked to change a bill. When he got out his pocket-book, the other just took it out of his hands. Amazed, he saw the situation and drew his pistol. A third accomplice came up. One of them pushed up his hand, and quietly told him to put that thing into his pocket, or he would get into trouble. Another then took his watch. Then they hustled him to the door, and told him the less fuss he made about it, the better it would be for him. The thirty minutes were nearly up, the bell rang, and all he could do was to grit his teeth, hurry back to the car, get aboard and leave."

"How much did he lose?"

"A hundred and eighty-five dollars, and a gold watch that he had just bought in San

Francisco." He then pointed out another man upon whom the runner had first tried his hand. He had accompanied him to the saloon, but suspected something wrong and prepared to use his bowie-knife. When the game was played, and he was politely asked to make change, he quietly moved toward the door, prevented the third man from cutting off his retreat, bowed himself out, and bade them good evening.

He then told me their simple method of operating. When the train comes up, it is just dark. The "roper-in" is on hand, dressed in full traveler's garb—felt hat, duster buttoned up to the neck, gloves of neatest fit, and a ticket sticking in his hat-band. As many eat no supper at all, or simply a lunch at a restaurant, they always find "game."

Then my own experience came to me with a hot flash. With that same rascal I had walked across that same square toward the open door of a restaurant, where a man vigorously rang a bell. This nice gentleman, with the daintiest boots, the finest gray alpaca duster buttoned up to his smooth neck, an elegant gray slouch, with a ticket in the band, conversed most agreeably as we walked over, and then invited me to go into the saloon, next door, and take a drink before eating. I replied that I was not at all thirsty. He urged me to come and take something with him—it would do me good. I then told him I was not in the habit of drinking, and paused for him to cross before me to the other door. He went his way, I mine. A dozen others came in for supper, and I wondered that that handsome gentleman with the neat kid gloves did not come, too. Whether he succeeded with somebody else, I do not know. There was no loss from our car, excepting a valise and an overcoat, stolen from near the door, while the owner was at supper. It was generally concluded that Sidney was a den of thieves, and if hard language could have brought the judgment of Sodom upon the place, there had been a conflagration before morning.

The Platte River is a peculiar stream. In

many places, it is more than a half mile wide, and, at a distance, looks as if it were deep. But its average depth, is said to be, not over *six inches!* And yet, if you attempt to cross, you may not find bottom at that many feet. In the early day it was the terror of emigrants and teamsters. Many is the wagon, and horse, and bullock, that have gone down in its treacherous quicksands.

At Omaha, we crossed the fine new bridge to Council Bluffs. From there, I came via St. Louis, crossing another magnificent bridge over the Missouri, at St. Charles. But the finest of all the bridges, is that over the Mississippi, at St. Louis. It is built of iron, and is supported by tubular arches. Two of the massive stone piers rest on the rock a hundred feet below the surface of the water; while more than a hundred feet above, is the broad avenue for local travel. Immediately beneath the wagon-way, is the railroad, which continues under the city by tunnel. In several respects it excels all other bridges in the world.

After spending a little time in St. Louis, I

visited a class-mate, ninety miles down the Mississippi, and thus enjoyed a little steamboat ride on this great river. From St. Louis home, seemed but a step. It was refreshing to see cultivated fields, once more, and groves of familiar trees.

As it is impossible to comprehend the vastness of the ocean without sailing across it, so it is impossible to appreciate the size of our country without traveling over it. And it is difficult even then. The man who would be most likely to fully comprehend it, is the man who drove from Maine to California in his own wagon. However, whether by steam or horsepower, the one who has crossed will not have the least doubt that "Uncle Sam is rich enough to give us all a farm." And yet, he may very reasonably doubt whether the recipient would be any richer for owning several farms, in some of the sections through which he has passed.

CHAPTER XI.

A FISHERMAN, wet, tired, and hungry, returning from a long tramp, was asked whether he had caught anything?

" Yes," was the brief reply.

" What?"

" A *cold!*"

If the writer were asked what he had gained, by his expedition to California, he might answer:

First—Considerable information concerning that remarkable State, and

Second—Improved physical health.

In regard to the first, the State is remarkable in several respects. Such are its people, its mineral and agricultural resources, its climate and its scenery. Of some of these, I have already expressed an opinion. Here may properly be added a few words, as to the inducements held out to immigrants.

Of climate, there is a great variety. In the Sacramento and San Joaquin Valleys, as well as in the Southern part of the State, it is hot and dry, from March until October. This is exceedingly favorable, both for gathering harvests and traveling on horseback. Of course, it necessitates irrigation for the later crops. This is generally done with moderate labor, and at reasonable expense. But not always.

To illustrate. Along the lower Kaweah, among the foot-hills, there was a fine little ranch, which I sometimes passed. Peach, apple, and apricot trees, potatoes and other vegetables, were flourishing very early in the spring. One day, one of the owners, with shovel in hand, was wading around in the mire with bare feet, and pantaloons rolled to his knees. I reined up to talk a little, and spoke of the splendid appearance of his orchard and garden.

"True," he replied, " but this is rough work; I got up this morning at five o'clock, came

18

out here and turned on the water, waded
around an hour in this cold mud, then went
in and held my feet under the stove, until
breakfast was ready. After breakfast, I got
at it again, and am at it yet."

I referred to some of the gardens down on
the plains, that were burning up, and remarked,
that he had the advantage of them, in having
plenty of water.

"Yes, there's water plenty, but, confound
it, I don't like to do my own raining."

His brief speech gave me a new revelation
of the power and weakness of man.

It was often a matter of surprise to me, that
there were so many poor people—people who
were making the barest living. Many had
been disappointed, and kept moving from
point to point. For a Californian to move,
seems to be about as little trouble, as for a
Bedouin to strike tent. Many have lived in
half a dozen counties and followed as many
occupations.

Southern California appeared to offer the
greatest advantages to men of small means.

But even there, it takes time to build up a home and secure independence. The semi-tropical fruits pay largely, when the orchards are ten or twenty years old. Few can wait so long. There are mouths to feed, bodies to clothe, trees, seeds, and implements to buy, and heavy taxes to pay, during long months and years, before there is any return. Some wisely rent farms and pay the rent in produce, until they are able to purchase. Others get disgusted, and soon roll out to a new spot, that, in the distance, looks more promising. Between the failures of crops, and the enormous rates of interest, which all are required to pay, many of the poor farmers are ground as fine, financially, as the grain they raise. Very often the crop sprouts and grows to maturity, under the shadow of a mortgage.

To those who go with plenty of capital, there is no trouble. Money loaned, invested in stock, or in real estate, is quite sure to bring ample returns. A comparatively few own magnificent estates. On the plains of the San Joaquin, you can ride along a half day, and every acre your horse traverses belongs to the same man.

Numbers have grown wealthy in raising cattle and sheep. The latter, especially, have proved a source of early profit to those of moderate means. Like land, they are often put out on the shares. If a poor man possesses the knowledge of properly handling them, his way to wealth is certain, if he steadily pursues it.

The mining is now nearly all done by large companies. A few Chinamen may be seen in the old deserted placer diggings. The sand, the gravel, and the boulders, that years ago rattled in the pan, the rocker, or the "long-tom" of the eager American miner, are now subjected to the patient scrutiny of the rice-eater. If he can pan out fifty cents per day, he gets rich, for he will board and clothe himself for one-third of that amount.

Taking everything together, and judging from what is everywhere evident, California repays the immigrant no better than the older States, east of the mountains. There is inspiration in her big trees, big fruits, and big farms. There is grandeur in her majestic mountains, and freedom from the rigor of eastern winters, in her sunny valleys. There is glitter in her gold, and electric speed in her business life. But to multitudes, she has proved a jeweled sorceress, in the beginning, promising crowns and palaces, and in the end, denying even a hat and hovel. The wrecks of her ruined fortune seekers strew the coast.

Others revel awhile in splendor, then lose all in reckless speculation, and finally scrape up a wretched living, in some menial occupation, or hide from insupportable misery in the cell of the felon, or in the grave of the suicide.

To the temperate, industrious, patient, and God fearing, she metes out the usual reward, viz: peace, honor, prosperity.

As to the healthfulness of the climate, there are various opinions. In different parts of the State, I found those whose health had been improved, especially, in Southern California. I met others who had reaped no advantage, and learned of others whose death seemed to have been hastened by going there. Many sick people too long delay to take rest. They take medicine, and work on, when they should do neither. No climate will work miracles.

So far as my own experience and observation go, the best medicines are fresh air, plain food, and exercise up to the point of weariness. Hunting in the mountains fills the prescription. To find mountains we need not travel far, either east or west. Those of California are especially favorable, as during so many months there is no rain. The ground, anywhere, furnishes a warm dry bed, the sky a magnificent tent, and a few blankets ample covering. The life is a rough one, but full of interest.

To any afflicted with vocal trouble, I would recommend a *whole bear*. Not that you take him, but that circumstances suddenly render it highly probable that he will take you. It will unearth any vocal talent you may have buried. A physician may safely recommend a medicine that has benefited himself.